One Spark

"Imagination Begins with You…" 2021

One Spark
"Imagination Begins with You…" 2021

Compiled by Brianna and Levi Teel

This is a compilation of works submitted by high school students for the "Imagination Begins with You..." annual writing contest. Each story's copyright is owned by the author of that story and used by permission in this compilation. All profits from this compilation will fund scholarships for higher education.

Library of Congress Control Number: 2020940635

Cover design by Jasmine Mumford

Interior design by Jasmine Mumford and Brian Claspell

ISBN: 978-1-947315-09-9

ACKNOWLEDGMENTS

Many people have helped judge and make this high school writing contest possible. The stories have been phenomenal.

We extend our thanks to all of the judges, to all of the teachers and administrators who encourage their students to participate, and to all of the students who send in the stories. We extend a special thanks to Brian Claspell, who has sponsored this competition, and without whom this contest would not be possible.

2021 Winners and Finalists

Winner:

Memories of You   by Kennedy Laney

Second Place:

Paper Birch   by Ayana Davies

Honorable Mentions:

An Unspoken Truce   by Kenneth Reed
To Be Brave Like You   by Isaac Lee Heidenblut
Serenity   by Kayla Freedman

Finalists:

"100 Mile Journey" By Jonathan Eisert

"6601" By Audrey Spillman

"A Cold War and a Crimson Ledger" By Shirley Lachance

"A Dark Halloween" By Alexia Davis

"A Passionate Lamentation" By Emma Khoury

"A Peek into the Future" By Reeja Khan

"Always Coming Back" By Ameena Ahmed

"Broken" By Ava Robinson

"Creux" By Carolina Herrera

"Crimson Winter" By Asa Handy

"Diamond Gate" By Krysta Even

"Drinking and Driving" By Yoset Reyes

"Eden of Igo" By Rosabella Debty

"Eternal Memory" By Ariyanna Donley

"False Dreams" By Abbie McCollum

"Flesh of Sin" By Elijah

"His Fair Lady" By Alexandra Price

"Homeless" By Lakyn Russell

"How I Grew to Love my Culture" By Melanie Antony

"In Perfect Unison" By Shelby Wharton

"In the Future" By Chad Jordan

"Malice" By Ryleigh Moule

"My Aspergian Arch-Nemesis" By Ian Cann

"Narcissus" By Diana Song

"Order" By Sam Mutschler-Aldine

"Our Struggles" By Lauren Christian

"Paper Mates" By Margaret Hahn

"Peanut and Carrot" By Daya Muldrow

"Pumpkin" By Mia Schramm

"Puzzle Pieces" By Prapthi Jayesh Sirrkay

"Quiet Familiarity" By Hannah Hoover

"Run" By Evelyn Rodriguez

"Shattered" By Maddie Martin

"Sin Island" By Caeden Conklin

"Stitches" By McKenna Mitcham

"The Alley" By Harrison Keeler

"The Deal" By Cliff Fraley

"The Decision that Changed my Life" By Steve Samson

"The Devil's Pawn" By Isabella Vasilides

"The Forbidden Marshmallows" By Abdul Cherchar

"The Huntress" By Ingrid Celis

"The Legend of the Tifflewick Brew" By Jace Ballard

"The Mat" By Corinne de Syon

"The Murk" By Cheyanna Xenos

"The Tale of The Starving Girl" By Lizzie Adams

"Tuatha Dé Danann" By Julaisa E. Santiago

"Viribus- A Story About Strength" By Gabriella Harris

"What Does It Feel Like To Be a Teenager?" By Paysen Hudson

"Will To Live" By Violet Mostek

"Woodrow West; The Cactus Dragon" By Aidan Evans

"Zemira" By Jacqueline Diehl

CONTENTS

Various Authors

SECTION 1 - FRIENDSHIP

Memories of You

By Kennedy Laney (2021 Winner)

She was the loudest trumpet player in the back of the class while I was the timid flute player in the front row. Every day at the start of fourth period, she'd walk in and immediately brighten the room with her smile. With her wavy caramel colored hair and big blue eyes, there was no overlooking her anywhere. One day before class had started, she came up to me and began talking up a storm. From that day forward, we were best friends who experienced crazy adventures together. From our daily lunch conversations to our endless jokes, there was never a dull moment when I was with her. Gracie, you were such a light in my life.

On January 1, 2018, when I got the call saying you had died, I sat in my room and cried for hours. You were only fourteen years old. Way too young to take your own life. You had so much ahead of you and big plans for the future. I cannot imagine what was going on that you felt this was the only solution. As I experienced all the emotions associated with a death, the one that resonated with me the greatest was guilt.

How could I have not known. Could I have done something different to change this path you were planning on taking? The rumors surrounding your death made the situation more difficult to deal with. I just did not understand.

Your candlelight vigil was beautiful; an entire church was filled with people who loved you and wore green in support of your family. The community and school tied ribbons around trees as a sign of remembrance. Tears streamed down hundreds of faces while pastors and friends shared stories of your time with us. I will never be able to fully understand what was going on in your life, but if I could go back to that day, it would be completely different. I would listen to you and talk you through whatever was happening. Suicide shouldn't have been an option. Heaven may have gained an angel that day, but I will miss you forever and always, Gracie Lynne.

It's been a little over three years since you left us. You are still not forgotten. Graduation is just around the corner and our senior class has already dedicated a seat for you to sit with us. You may not be here physically, but you will always be in our heart and in our minds.

Paper Birch

By Ayana Davies (2021 Second Place)

Another morning comes. The ocean laps upon the receding shoreline, and I stand there, alone once again. The sun rises from the rolling waves and paints the water's surface various shades of orange and yellow. Dirt falls from the cliffside and tumbles into the water with small ripples. My roots jut out from the cliff face in some places and bury deep in others.

My time is coming soon. I desperately hold onto dirt and soil, but time will take what it wants, no matter my wishes. My brothers and sisters all met the same fate and have dispersed themselves into the ocean below. I am growing older. I am already pushing borrowed time. I am next.

Something comes. They stand on two feet and cover themself in sheets of purple and blue. Brown hair sprouts from the top of their head and lightly covers the rest of their body. I've seen these before. They're spry and noisy usually. They're quiet today. It's an interesting change. I watch them pluck a flower by my root. I'm glad that they aren't larger than me, and I'm grateful that I'm not a flower.

"It's an awfully gorgeous day out. What do you think?" I've never been spoken to, at least, not that I remember. It is a very pretty day. The sky is clear; the water below is kinder today.

"I think you'd like this, huh, Willow? Said you always wanted to visit again." Ah, so I wasn't being spoken to. I'm glad I can't respond in that case. It would have been awfully awkward.

I remember that name though. There was another one of them here once. I remember the one who's below me now too. This one is named Jaime. Jaime was tall and loud. They seemed headstrong, and always led the way. Willow was smaller and frailer, but just as boisterous. They were both much shorter then too, and I was only a few rings wide. Their hair was short and messy, stuffed full with leaves and blades of grass. They both climbed on me decades ago and leaped off of me like they were fledglings. The branch they snapped off back then is still shorter than the others. I remember that those two were close.

I remember their voices. They were squeaky and high pitched, but filled with energy and excitement. It changed as they grew taller. Their foreign noises became deeper and more confident. On some days they screamed loud enough to rival the sea. They wrestled and shouted, then laughed it off as they tumbled down the hill. Their words were meaningless at first, but slowly I learned what their noises meant: when they were angry and when they were sad. Basic emotions and sounds slowly became complex thoughts, and single words became full sentences. I could never catch everything, but I learned all that I knew from my silent watching. On some days they were quieter, or they said nothing. They flipped through small, thick, and bound sheets of white and black text, and leaned on each other in near silence. Those sheets had a strange familiarity to them, though I could never pin it.

I remember the patterns they wore. The first few years were filled with colors bright enough to rival the spring flowers. As time moved on, they dulled. They wore more patterns, less patterns. In winter evenings, they would come hidden under green and grey fur sheets, and giggle while sipping from steam filled cups. The colors would come back in the summer months, but with each year they slowly faded to more neutral hues.

I remember the last time I saw them together. Willow and Jaime were as tall as I had ever seen them. They spoke too quickly for me to understand, but I could hear their hurt tones. They weren't angry or sad. It was both, I suppose, and water traced their cheeks by the time they left together, hands clasped and holding each other near.

Willow occasionally came after that, always alone. They tended to visit most in the first place, though their visits became even more sparse. They were pale and huffing with each visit, but always made the trek up the hill. They slept under me some nights and would walk back before morning would come. The last day they ever came, they stayed at my roots until the sun rose. It was just before the afternoon before others came to retrieve them.

I remember the silence. Days between visits turned to months, to years. Decades of serenity and sameness. There were minute differences in the days that passed, but nothing as significant as the dozens of conversations that happened below me. I am here now though, and for the day I am back to those noisy years. I see Jaime now, and time has treated them relatively well. Their face has small creases and streaks of light hair can be seen towards the back of their hair. Still, they look young. They have much more time than I do.

Jaime is still talking to Willow. They reminisce on memories I have buried deep within me. I recognize all of the moments they speak about, the tears that return to their cheeks, and the heavy sigh they release. It feels like I'm listening in on something personal, but they let the silence sit between us for the rest of their time here. They nap, they read. They look to a bright box in hand when the sun begins to set, then leave. The tide has risen. It is my subtle reminder that my time has come closer. It reminds me that I do not have forever.

Despite the monotony of watching the same waters pass below, there is always something new, no matter how insignificant. A leaf falls, a caterpillar changes, the wind blows differently, an old voice says a new goodbye. This is a new day.

It is a nice day.

An Unspoken Truce

By Kenneth Reed (Finalist and Honorable Mention)

"Come on, George, it'll be our time, we'll be heroes!" Butch exclaimed to his best friend of about 13 years now. George and Butch had met at the age of 7, when Butch had started a schoolyard brawl in order to fend off the local "fresh meat" harvesters from George.

"Hold on, Butch, Ma told me to come home for lunch." George said to Butch, already backpedaling towards his Alabama home. He strode into the kitchen to greet his mother, but was instead greeted by his father sitting at the kitchen table with an army recruiter.

"Hello, Mr. Williams, I'm Lt. Colonel Greene, and I'm here to congratulate you on your admittance into the United States Armed Forces." George was speechless. He had been wanting this for a long time, ever since Butch had told him about his Uncle fighting in the Civil War.

"He was a hero! Killed as many Yanks as there are hairs on your head. Now, it's our turn to do that to the Hun." War had been declared in August about three years ago after that archduke guy, Ferdinand something, George wasn't too sure. Marines had landed in July of last year, in 1916, and now, he was getting a chance to fight.

"Um, thank you sir, I appreciate it...uh, sir." George wasn't sure what to say. The recruiter left, and George and his family had lunch, celebrating his new recruitment.

"At twenty years old, George, you'll make a fine soldier, son," his father said.

The following months went by fast, especially after George got into the rhythm of boot camp. By the time October came, George was being deployed. His last days before being shipped to the Western Front were spent at home. He found out then that Butch had been recruited too. He went to a completely different boot camp, but was being shipped to the same location: Verdun, France.

His last day at home, he spent on the bench in front of the corner store, people watching. He saw an old woman pulling a wagon full of children. He watched as her bag of groceries ripped from the bottom and the food spilled out onto the ground. She cursed like a sailor, and one of the children mimicked the strange sounds coming out of their grandmother's mouth.

Butch came up behind him and grabbed his shoulders.

"You ready to kill you some Huns, George?" he said, as he sat down next to him.

"I'm gonna miss this place, Butch." George replied, still staring at the old woman.

"Of course you are, everyone misses home every once in a while. Just know that you're fighting to keep your home safe."

October had come and gone, and with it, November, December, and January. The Allies had begun to push the Western Front back into Germany. Their next assault was on the town of Arras. Butch and George were waiting for their captain to order them into the city when the battle started. That's exactly what happened. A tide of brown and grey surged towards the city, and soon, the tide became brown, grey, and red. British, French, and American soldiers breached the city and began to take control. There was a field immediately east of the town, filled with craters and trenches from artillery fire. That's where George and Butch found themselves.

"George! Gimme one of your grenades!" Butch shouted. George gave him the stick with explosives on the end, and as he poked his head out of the trench, a bullet passed through his esophagus, and the lit grenade dropped onto the ground, inches from George. George scrambled backwards and covered his neck and head with his arms. When the grenade exploded, a piece of shrapnel pierced his leg.

He suddenly decided he'd had enough. He jumped out of the trench and hobbled toward the woods to the east. Bullets hit the ground around him, spraying dirt into his face. He finally made it to the woods, and kept going until he found a creek and leaped (as best he could) into it. He landed in the water and put his back against the bank, finally safe from gunfire. Or so he thought.

George heard the bolt of a rifle slam back and spun around like a top. He saw a German soldier with the single spike on his helmet pointing his rifle at him. But, for some reason, he didn't shoot. George took this advantage and snatched up his rifle and pointed it at the German.

Both men stood for a moment, pointing their rifles at each other. George sensed that there was no hostility coming from the German. He slowly lowered his rifle, and so did the German.

"Hi. I'm George", he said.

"Wilhelm", the German said in return. Both men sat down on the bank, both eyeing each other, in case either one of them decides to suddenly change his mind about being not hostile.

George reached out his arm with his canteen in hand.

"Water?"

"Nein, I have some." Wilhelm said.

"You don't really want to be here, do you?" George asked.

"Not really, no. I had been conscripted only a few months ago. I was ripped away from my children like a chicken away from its egg."

"I'm sorry you had to leave your family behind."

"Family? Oh no, I don't have a family. The children were a part of my daycare center. I always loved seeing innocent faces filled with pure joy. It filled me with compassion, not hostility. You don't want to be here, either, no?"

"Right. I thought I did. Wanted to kill some Hun. That's how my buddy Butch put it. But he's...he's..."

"I understand."

Tears began to fall down George's cheeks. The death of Butch had just hit him like a truck.

"It was supposed to be a big adventure. They told us we would be fighting for the greater good, that the Hun had it coming." George looked at Wilhelm and saw that he was crying as well. I guess neither of us got what we were promised. The two men exchanged stories of how Wilhelm helped a child through his mother's death, and how George had saved his little brother from bullies as Butch had done him. After a half hour or so, they heard the water further downstream begin to splash. Wilhelm and George got up tried to hide but it was too late. Three German soldiers had somehow escaped the battle, and were searching for a way to counter-attack. The Allies had won.

"Wilhelm! What are you doing!" One of them shouted.

"Um, I-" Wilhelm didn't get to finish, as the German soldier pulled his pistol out of his holster and pointed it at George. Wilhelm shouted and jumped in front of George as soon as the bullet left the chamber. The bullet hit Wilhelm right under his heart. He began to gasp and stutter, then fell backwards into George. They all heard shouting from just over the ridge. It was the Allies.

The German soldiers sprinted back down, the creek, leaving George be.

"Help! Someone help!" Wilhelm grabbed George's hand.

"They will not help a random German soldier. They do not know me as you do. Thank you , George." The last bit of life slipped out of Wilhelm as his hand splashed down into the water. Some Allied soldiers came into view and saw George standing above the dead German.

"Nice! You got one!" One of them yelled.

"Uh, yeah…yeah, sure did."

"Did you see any others?"

"Um…no, no I didn't, he was the only one." George said.

The war lasted until November of 1918, however George was allowed to return home that summer. He sat on the same green bench in front of that same old corner store, watching the same old people.

He saw the same old lady walking with the same children, but they were walking, rather than being tugged along. All of a sudden, the bag ripped and her groceries fell on the ground. George leapt up, and jogged towards the old lady, and helped pick up her groceries, and even offered to pay for some more.

"Oh, that's alright, Young Man, I appreciate that, though. I'm getting a bit too old for this." The only thing he saw in his mind as the lady walked down the street with her grandchildren was Wilhelm, and his daycare full of children, masked by the evil that was created around the Hun.

Serenity

By Kayla Freedman (Finalist and Honorable Mention)

Franklin pulled into the garage of the house and turned off the ignition of his old, rusty green car. He hobbled out of seat, closed the door, and locked the doors behind him. He climbed up the steps of the house, using the railing for support. At his age, he was one fall away from death. His shaky hands reached for the knob and he flung the door wide open, peering inside. Everything was just how it was the last time he was there, and yet everything felt different. Franklin walked into the tiny bathroom near the door. His hands grasped the sides of the sink and his head slowly lifted. His eyes glared into the mirror, analysing his reflection. His eyes were dark and empty. There wasn't a spark like there used to be. His face was wrinkly and saggy. His pruney fingers rustled through his hair, which was thin and balding. His shoulders were tense and his eyebrows were furrowed. He didn't recognize himself. It was terrifying. A tear slid down his face.

The beach house was Franklin's favorite place in the world. Franklin and Ava would travel up there every summer in that very same green car. They would sing songs and laugh until they couldn't breathe. They would ride bikes on the boardwalk and eat ice cream. Franklin loved chocolate and Ava loved vanilla. They would lounge on the beach and chase seagulls. They lived in a dream. They were perfect together. Everyone said so. It's very rare to meet your perfect soulmate in your lifetime, but Franklin and Ava had found each other. This year, Ava passed away. Franklin didn't believe their time was coming to an end. He refused to accept it. He misses her more than anyone has ever missed anyone. She was his reason for living.

He made it out to the porch of the house. He took in the ocean air and felt the wind shuffle through his cardigan. He carefully sat down in one of the purple chairs they had put out on the porch a few years back. He wished Ava was sitting next to him, laughing at him, teasing him, kissing him. He turned back towards the view and let out a long breath. He began to bawl. Tears and snot streamed down his face as he gripped his heart. It hurt too much.

Suddenly, he heard sounds of music. He looked down towards the end of the porch and saw the windchimes. Ava found them at a market and told him that she had to have them. The windchimes were made of glass and they moved like magic. The glass was serenity blue, which was Ava's favorite shade of blue. She had favorite shades of each color. She was special like that. He helped himself up and approached the windchimes. The wind made them dance like crazy and Franklin smiled. He let his shoulders relax and he took out his handkerchief to wipe off his tears. He leaned up against the white railing off the porch and watched the windchimes.

Franklin found it calming. He tried to practice his breathing exercises that his therapist had taught him to do. The windchimes brought him back to a place with Ava. He imagined her laughing with her mouth open and milk squirting out of her nose. It was her dancing even with no music on. He imagined her finding the windchimes at the market and setting them up on the porch. He opened his eyes because the music had stopped. The day had become peaceful and the wind was gone. He studied the still chimes. The color was soft and beautiful, and he realized why Ava loved it so much.

Franklin knew in his heart that Ava would never have wanted this for him. In fact, she would slap him if she saw him as depressed as he was now. But the hardest thing was to accept that she's gone. He thinks everyday she's going to wake up beside him and life will carry on like before. But as he touched the soft blue glass, he felt closer to Ava than he had in a long time. In that moment, he was the most at peace that he could have been. Acceptance is not a stage Franklin wanted to go through. It would mean she was really gone. But just for that split second, he lived in a state of tranquility, and a state of peace. He knew it wouldn't last forever. He held onto Ava's favorite thing, because she was his favorite thing. He started to cry again but it was different. The tears were happy. He was going to get through this.

Paper Mates

By Margaret Hahn (Finalist)

I remember it like it was yesterday. She arrived as they all do, in packs of two or three. Excited for what her future held and giggling with her friends about the things she might do and see. She had the most beautiful black hair pulled back into a chic ponytail and the most beautiful face I'd ever seen. Her name was Sharpay and she was the love of my life.

My name is Patrick, Pat for short. I'm your standard run of the mill mechanical pencil. Manufactured in a big warehouse with millions of others who look just like me. Being that I'm a mechanical pencil I'm basically immortal, get me a few pieces of lead and I'm good as new. Most of the other tools on the desk think I'm weird. I'm mostly used for notes and homework so no one really gets me. Oh, except for the highlighters but even then they only know random blurts of information, whereas I'm more well rounded. I digress, point is I'm kind of a loner. But that all changed when she arrived.

Sharpay was different from most pens who entered the studio. She wasn't loud and boisterous as other pens and markers. She was more sophisticated and withdrawn. But best of all she LOVED art. Sharpay was a fine point pen used for detailed, intricate pieces of art. She focused on every small detail most would deem insignificant to the bigger picture. She knew how to look past the bigger picture and into the story within. Since Sharpay and I had two completely different jobs I never really got to talk to her, but I admired her from afar. She was so dedicated to her work. It was truly inspiring.

One day, when the Scribe wasn't home, I got up the courage to cross over to the art side of the desk to get a closer look at one of her pieces. She was working on a larger piece and had just begun the details on the face. She captured the emotions so beautifully. Every line, every crevasse, every hair on this face was just as it should be. I was so enthralled by the image when all of a sudden, TAP! TAP!

I spun around to see Sharpay looking at me. I didn't know what to say or do.

"Admiring my work I see." she said cooly.

"Oh yes. It's very pretty." I responded quickly. She stood there for a minute, pondering her work.

"Hm, I dunno. I just feel like something's missing." she replied, focusing hard on the piece. I stood beside her and looked as well.

"Maybe if you did something like this?" I said and before I knew it I found myself sketching away at this beautiful work of art. I was shocked at myself but continued to draw as I couldn't seem to stop.

Once I finished I turned to look at Sharpay. Her face was shocked and it seemed as if she couldn't move. Horrified that I might have offended her I quickley exclaimed, "I'm sorry! I'm sorry! I didn't mean to ruin your work! Don't worry, I'll erase this mess right away!"

"NO!" she called out, "That's just what it needed!"

She hurried over and began to trace over what I had made until every little sketch mark was overlaid with her pristine black lines.

We both stood back to look at what we had made. It was perfect. Sharpay looked over at me.

"I don't believe we've met before?" she stated.

"No, we wouldn't have. I'm a part of the work side of the desk, you're on the art side." I informed her.

She stood for a little while contemplating my words before saying, "Well, perhaps you're on the wrong side of the desk" before turning to walk back to her station.

I stood there for a minute before turning to run after her, "Wait! Sharpay!"

"Yes?" she responded a little startled.

"I, um, would it be ok if we kept drawing together?" I asked.

She looked at me for a minute before responding.

"I'd like that." she replied with a smile.

After that day, Sharpay and I began to secretly draw together. I would sketch something out and we would work on it together until we had come up with a piece that we both like. We made so many beautiful pieces together, but like all good things, our time together came to an untimely end.

You see unlike a mechanical pencil, a pen is not immortal and does not last forever. While we were making all this art together, Sharpay was wearing herself out faster and faster with each elegant stroke. One day it was just too much.

When I arrived that night I found her friends huddled around her empty station. When I asked what had happened, they told me that Sharpay had used so much of her ink making work with me that when the Scribe was trying to ink an image they had used so much pressure to get the ink out that it had crushed Sharpay's tip and the Scribe threw her away.

I was horrified. It couldn't be true! But when I ran out onto the desk floor I had seen it was. There was the paper the Scribe had been using and there in the middle of the paper was the last ink blot from Sharpay.

I cried and mourned her for weeks, even contemplated throwing myself away, but what good would that do. Eventually I made my piece with the past and came to terms that Sharpay was gone. I still have every piece of art we made together. Whenever I get sad I look at them and think about the time we shared together and the love I still have for her. My Paper Mate.

Always Coming Back

By Ameena Ahmed (Finalist)

Stray dogs have a habit of always coming back, unwanted or not.

Every day, the boy would wake up, tie his cloak tight around him, and take the long walk down to the village. He was a young child who couldn't be older than twelve years old. Nobody in the village knew his exact age, he was an enigma to all of them. It's contradictory really- ostracized by people who didn't know why they didn't like him. But he looked wrong and acted wrong, so that was reason enough.

Everyone kept a distance from the moment he was in diapers and kept at it. It might have been his refusal- or inability - to speak that angered the elders. It may have been the large birthmark that covered half of his face that made the other parents hide their children as he walked by. The boy was unassuming to all of this. He overcompensated to make others feel more comfortable around him, walking through the village with his hood covering his face and his shoulders hunched. If he covered his face they wouldn't throw him harsh glares. Sometimes he'll get a fresh loaf of bread from a pitying baker if he loiters around long enough. It warmed his cold hands but didn't do much for his sandpaper mouth. On his back he carried firewood he'd collect from the surrounding woods and continued down the narrow trails to the opposite end of the village.

"You're late, boy" a gruff voice spoke up as he walked in.

The boy clutched the straps of the bag on his bag, sucking in a breath. Today his friend looked worse. Every day he slumped further in his chair and talked less. The man speaking to him was old and lived far from the other dwellings. He was the first person the young boy had a memory of, and he's the only one who speaks to him. The boy has never had any other friends. From sneaking glances on his walks, he'd see kids his age chasing each other around and playing ball. Attempting to play with them never worked out, but it was alright. He had one friend who liked him just fine.

He slowly walked up to the fireplace and set down the wood. The boy made quick work to sweep the floors, the sounds of the creaking wood filling the quiet room. He paused when a sickening cough racked through his friend. He kept sweeping though because his friend didn't like to see him sick. Shame, that was the word the man used.

After sweeping and setting the fireplace ablaze, he dragged a chair to sit next to his friend by the window. Today he was wrapped in two blankets, chin lowered as his white hair covered most of his face. At times like this when he wasn't looking, the boy liked to take a moment to look long and hard at his friend.

23

Wrinkles and rashes didn't cover up the large birthmark on the man's face. The boy liked it though because it made them have something in common. He picked up the extra loaf of bread he got from a baker today and set it down on the table between them. The old man was always doing things for him, whether it was building him his tiny shed on the other side of the village, slipping him silver coins every week, or inviting him here on cold days like this.

Although the boy was young, he wasn't unfamiliar with death. Diseases were common around the village, sure, but he has seen some of the elders pass away, carried away in open caskets as the villagers came one by one to pay their respects. His friend was older than any of the village elders though, and with each passing day, he grew more and more sickly.

"Good fired wood today," his friend said, clearing his throat. The boy looked up from cutting the loave in half, eagerly nodding. He was happy that his friend noticed. The thought of leaving the home later to his friend sitting in the same chair, alone with a cold fireplace made him anxious. Getting good firewood wasn't hard, so he made the extra effort.

The man's thoughts were going down a similar path. The thought of this young boy coming home to him one day, trying to wake him up to no avail, left him anxious. He has regrets, like letting the boy live on the other side of the village, thinking it would harden him for when the man eventually did pass away. If he could go back, he would have invited him to live with him, sheltering him from the harshness of the village. But it's too late for all of that now. The boy will come here one day to find a cold fireplace and his friend gone. He will poke around the creaky home, cleaning up the dust that collected overnight.

After, he will sit by the window, bread in hand, just like he would if his friend were still there. Then he will live here, in his friend's home, sitting with silent tears.

He's kind of like a stray dog in that way, always coming back.

In Perfect Unison

By Shelby Wharton (Finalist)

The great old oak tree stood tall and contemptuous. When he arose from his sleep he stretched his leaves and branches and shook them, knocking the mother of five who had just begun to rest after finishing her nest. Startled and course the blue mama jay checked her children then promptly spoke to the old tree. "Now what would prompt you to awake and knock a sleeping mother and her children!" The blue jay said sharply. The oak tree acted as if he could not hear her at first, only until he realized she had not gone and awaited an answer from the tree, he lowered himself domineeringly and said,

"You are not fit to sleep in my branches." He spoke in a calm yet harsh manner. Then raised himself once again. "And why is that?" the blue jay pondered.

"You have more than enough room for my children and I, wouldn't you agree sir?"

"Indeed" the tree began, " however my branches are

reserved for only myself, now go on so I continue my slumber little bird."

Defeated by the great oak tree, the blue jay packed up her children and herself, In search of a new home. The mama jay had a total of five children, 3 of which were boys, and two girls. She named them the following, Tuck, Turner, Tanner, Taylor, and Tiana. They walked behind their mother in a triangle. The focal point set on the mother, they had walked for two days. They had yet to find a new home. "Mom, why can't we just fly?" whined Turner.

"Because Tiana hasn't learned yet" explained his mother.

"Well that's not our fault." Tuck added "She could do it if she just tried." He continued.

The chatter awoke a nearby tree. She was small and thin, and only had a few branches. The small tree opened her eyes to see the six sleepy birds. "Why hello there." The seeding said with a smile that seemed excited and a little afraid.

"What are you all doing out in this weather? It's too cold for you guys to be walking about." stated the small tree.

"We are looking for a new home, we got thrown out of our last one." the mama jay explained.

"Yeah, we had a really nice one until this big mean ol' tree kicked us out. He said we wasn't good enough to sleep there." Taylor said despairingly.

"I think I know what tree you're talking about. The great big oak tree with the big branches?" asked the seedling

"That's the one." said Tuck

"Oh yeah. He is pretty well known in the tree community for not allowing nice birds as yourself to nest in his branches. He is a piece of work."

"You got that right." Tiana said in a small quiet voice. She stood behind her mother at all times. Tiana was a shy bird, who never spoke to anyone outside of her family, Except this tree. Her brothers and sisters stood in shock.

"Well if you guys want, you can sleep in my branches. I know I don't have big branches, or as many. But I have a few and you can sleep in them." said the seedling. The mama jay paused for a moment, looked at the seedling and her branches, then at her tired children.

"We would be honored." Mama jay said in a clam and content voice. The six birds climbed into the small branches of the seedling and began to sleep, knowing that they had found a home and new friend. They slept with a feeling of harmony. And lived on with the tree as they all grew in perfect unity.

Our Struggles

By Lauren Christian (Finalist)

In the background soft music is playing, the same sad tune over and over again. I am rocking slowly side to side, nursing the tears that sit patiently on my eyelids but I refuse to let them fall. I'm tired, but I force myself to stay awake because the more my eyes hurt, the more I feel that I am still alive. It's 2:00 am and I am just sitting here thinking about my life, when my twin sister comes into our room from a late night party. My twin sister Gwendolyn is beautiful, she and I are identical twins but somehow she has all of the characteristics that I can only dream of. She comes into our room and I quickly lay down, and pretend that I'm asleep. Drowned in the darkness of night, and in the depth of my sadness, I just disappeared. Awoken by Gwendolyn, who reminded me that we had to get ready for school, I get in the shower and don't even wash my body or hair. I just stand there and let the steaming water beat my skin and the crown of my head. I step out of the shower and absentmindedly get dressed as I walk down the street and start to jog out of my neighborhood. I pass all of the dark green loaming trees and then cross the river leading into the forest, and find my secret place. I climb the rock and lit up a cigarette, I breath it in and let the smoke swirl in my body, and allow it to flow out of my nose. I let the breeze kiss my face and run its hands through my hair, as I looked up at the sky and I felt it open up. A single drop took out my cigarette and I smiled at how the rain spit on me, blowing me this way and that. For once in my life, the thunder that boomed around me and the lightning that flashed in front of me, made me want to live. A place so peaceful didn't deserve a human being that was so unstable. I climbed down from the rock and trudged back to my house so that I could regretfully get to school.

I arrived back at my house and let the silence of an empty house take me over. I go back to my room and find a pair of sweats that I throw on. Grabbing my bike, I start riding towards the school and I arrive at the end of our third block right before lunch. Texting my friend to open one of the side doors, I am met by Greyson who wraps his arms around me. Greyson pulls me into the building, and then pushes me down the next hallway, and outside so that we can sit behind the school in peace. Once we get outside, I realize, even through the cloudy skies that Greyson is mad. His face is set in stone and his jaw is flexing so much that I can tell his teeth have been grinding against each other all day. But his eyes, the most telling factor out of his entire face tell me a story, rage is battling inside him and he has been waiting to release this dam to someone he trusts. I lead him to our favorite spot under the willow tree where no one can find us, and we take a seat on the roots that have protruded out from under the Earth. His breathing becomes ragged and he soon is gasping for air, he can't breathe, he wants to but he can't. And thereafter the tears fall and his bony shoulders are shaking with anger and fear, and pain. I get up and I hold Greyson in my arms and he latches on to me as if I'm the life jacket that will save him from drowning. I hold him, as tight as I can, and chant the same words over and over to him, until he calms down. We sit like that and we rock as he cries and slowly but surely does he start to breathe again, and the only noise between us is the occasional sniffle from his nose.As he pulls back and combs his hair with his fingers, I see a slip of red marking on his wrist peeking out from under his sweatshirt sleeve.

"Grey, please tell me you didn't." I plead.

He looks up at me and sniffles but his eyes tell me everything I need to know before he even answers.

"I'm sorry I was so hollow inside, I didn't know what to do and I didn't want to call you because I knew that you were dealing with your own problems."

"Grey, if we're going to do this together then you have to stop, and I do too. Please. You can't keep doing this to yourself. Let me see both of your arms."

He extended both of his arms towards me and I gingerly rose up the sleeves of the sweatshirt. And there facing me was the angry, deep and jagged cuts of skin on his wrists. The jagged lines rose almost all the way up his arm, but they disappeared half way on his arm. They told me of a story of how desperate Greyson was to feel alive. So he picked up a silver marker and used his arms as the canvas and made art appear through deep, angry, and delicate swirls. I touched the sides where the skin was red and raw. So sensitive was his skin, but he so recklessly cared for it.

31

"Greyson, what have they done to you?" I searched his eyes for his response but he held his eyes down, because he knew he was already defeated.

"Everything, but nothing can stop the pain, quite like this." He whispered, and then he looked up at me and smiled.

Diamond Gate

By Krysta Even (Finalist)

A deafening roar fills my ears and overwhelms my senses. The seat I inhabit vibrates beneath me as I try to comprehend where I am and how I got here. The increased pounding of my heart pulses in my ears as loud as the engine. As I begin to adjust to this new setting, the sound of panicked breathing of others with the same fate as I, fills the cockpit. Stress induced perspiration slowly gathers at my temples and rolls down my checks. Air is sucked from the cabin as the door is raised, flooding the space with sunlight. I scan the room and run through scenarios of how we all arrived here and how I know these people. A high-pitch crackle comes over the intercom.

A friendly voice echoed off the walls, "Welcome to the survival scholarship, you must now decide if you are willing to endure the wilderness and be the first to reach the diamond gate. Some of you may not be up to the task and will be eliminated from the race. You have an hour to locate and enter the gate. Decide now and jump when the green lights flash if you are willing. Good Luck". I clutch the cords to my parachute. Fear emanates from the other passengers as we look into each other's eyes and know our time to jump is about to come. "Can I do this?" I contemplated. I had no experience surviving in the wild other than watching survival shows on tv occasionally and did not know if I would even be able to locate the gate.

As I was about to give up and take my seat again, I felt a hand on my shoulder, I turned around and was greeted by a familiar face. "Jake!" I squealed as I flung my arms around him. He stumbled backwards and chuckled as he stabilized. I pulled back and looked up at him in shock, "What are you doing here?" I whispered. He grabbed my arm and pulled me to the edge of the plane as the lights began flashing green meaning it was now time to jump. All he did was look back and smile before he pulled me over the edge sending us tumbling to the world below.

I gripped his hand as tight as I could in fear that if I let go, I would never be able to find him again. As we got near the ground, we were suddenly jolted backward with so much force the air was ripped from my lungs. Our parachutes had opened, and we were now slowly descending to the ground. Squinting I attempted to look as far into the distance as I could while I had the vantage point. In the distance I saw a sparkling like nothing I had ever seen before. It was nearly blinding as the sunlight reflected. I squeezed Jakes hand and looked over only to see him staring in awe as well. As it slipped from view, I attempted to map out the terrain. We would soon land on the river that cut the land in two. The rolling hills would need to be crossed.

The ground was coming closer and Jake shouted at me to start running. I felt silly but I started running as hard as I could with nothing but air below my feet but quickly that air turned to thick grass and my hand slipped from Jakes grip as we rolled. Once we stopped rolling, I quickly took off my parachute and backpack beginning to rummage through what was inside. Finding a small pencil and scrap of paper I began sketching out the tall hills and stretching river That would lead us to the diamond gate. Just as I finished sketching, Jake came up to me with sticks protruding from his hair. I couldn't help but laugh. He pointed at me and I noticed the leaves and twigs also tangled into my hair. He looked at my map and patted me on the back confessing, "I knew I needed you more than you needed me. When I saw you in the plane, I was so relieved. We must work together, to make it to the gate in time."

We quickly began deconstructing the parachute and taking all the string and tarp, stuffing it into our bags to use later. We made the quick walk down the hill and made it to the river. All along the river there were other kids, some alone and others in groups all trying to cross. Many tried to swim across, but the river was so wide that before the even made it halfway they turned and swam back to shore. I looked around, saw large logs and knew I needed to build a raft. Jake gathered the logs and tied them together using the string from the parachute. The tarps were attached to the logs and packed tightly with sand. We used twigs as paddles as we pushed the raft into the water and started paddling. The raging current was pulling us down the river. We had to be quick and each move was calculated and intentional. As we were paddling, I looked back and noticed the other kids running back to their parachutes to copy our raft. However, it was too late. We had a head start. When we reached the other side, we rushed through the grass to the gate. It was shining like a beacon begging us to hurry.as the gate slowly closed. "Run!" I screamed at Jake who was just behind me. We leapt over the threshold and looked back just as the gate closed. We turned around when heard leaves crumbling on the floor beneath the foot of the person who was walking towards us. She greeted us saying, "I am impressed with you using each other's strengths to your advantage." She was right, with my problem solving and Jakes strength we were able to succeed.

His Fair Lady

By Alexandra Price (Finalist)

The sun is there during the day, evening, and even the earliest of mornings. But while she is there most of the day, she also disappears from time to time. When that happens, instead of thanking her for working so hard during all that time, she is scorned for not being there when we cannot see her. And when she appears once again in the morning, she is bullied back into submission for she brings too much heat and brightness during the day. As the seasons come and go and there is little of her in the winter, the people mourn and moan for her warmth, but she hides away, unloved and degraded. Even while she works, the people do not appreciate her blinding radiance, only using her for what they may need. But when she has gone away, even with millions of miles between her and humanity, she can still feel the hatred pounded onto her every night and day. And when summer comes once more, when the heat rains down, when the brightness pierces through, she is rejected once again for all that she does.

There was one soul that loved her, though. The man of the moon. He saw her pain, and, when she got to her breaking point, he rescued her from the abuse. He offered an eclipse to shield her from the people and every night offered her a reprieve from the hurt as she hid away. The man, cherished as he was, loved her. He would reflect the brightness that radiated off her, and, as humanity watched him shine bright, the people would not realize that the light came from the one they tore down. The one that illuminated the sky throughout the day by herself, and through the night with help, even as they had brought only pain and burdens upon her. And as the people admired the man of the moon, he merely smiled his crescent white glow towards his fair lady that was the light of his world.

Peanut and Carrot

By Daya Muldrow (Finalist)

Once upon a time, there lived an Elephant named Peanut and a bunny named Carrot. They were great friends. They enjoyed reading, taking naps, but their favorite thing to do together is blowing bubbles. One day, when Carrot and Peanut were playing together outside. Some bunnies came over and invited Carrot to play but not Peanut. Carrot me the kind hearted bunny she is, went to join them. Poor Peanut had to play all by himself. Days passed, Carrot was still playing the bunnies and not Peanut. One of the days when Carrot and the bunnies were playing tea party, Pumpkin asked Carrot why she played with Peanut. "He is so different from you. How could you ever be friends with him?" She asked her. Instead of answering, Carrot decided to drink her tea and keep quiet. Carrot started thinking to herself why she was friends with Peanut. He is an elephant and I'm a bunny, she thought to herself. Meanwhile, Peanut was thinking of all the good memories of him and Carrot. He really did miss playing with her, he wished she would play with him again. Days later it was Pumpkin's birthday party and every bunny around was going. During the party though Carrot noticed that there were only bunnies at the party. She thought that wasn't right, she had enough of the bunnies not including other animals. Carrot called everyone outside, she walked over to a pond and everyone followed her. "Guys, you should be kind to everyone no matter how different they are from you. We all live in this world together, there is no reason we should be mean to each other" She said picking up a baby duck. "Maybe we should play with the other animals" one of the bunnies responded. "No, we are bunnies, we don't play with low class animals!" Pumpkin yelled. "Now Carrot I think it's time for you to go, you'll never be a real bunny". With that Carrot said her goodbyes and headed home. The next Carrot went to her mother for some advice about Peanut. "Honey, just go talk to him, he is your friend after all. I'm sure he misses you as much as you miss him. You could talk to him during the school play" her mother suggested. "That's a great idea mom, thank you" Carrot announced. During the school play Pumpkin yelled at Candy, a zebra to get off the stage. Candy was the only non-bunny in the play. That's when Carrot hopped out of her seat and ran on stage. "That's enough! When I was playing with you bunnies all you guys did was put down other animals. Stop hating on other animals just because they aren't bunnies! It's rude, mean and I'm not going to let it happen anymore. Also you want to know why Peanut is my friend Pumpkin? He is my friend because he isn't a bully like you, he is caring and fun to be around. I love Peanut with all my heart!" Carrot said. After she was done everyone gave her a round of applause. She hopped off stage and went over to her Peanut. "I'm sorry for the way I treated you Peanut. It was wrong of me, I hope you can forgive me." She said. "Yes of course I can!" he answered. "Hey Carrot, I wanted to thank you for opening up my eyes. I really was being a bully, for now on I will be nicer" Pumpkin declared. "I'm happy to hear that," Carrot said.

The End

Various Authors

SECTION 2 – BRAVERY

To Be Brave Like You

By Isaac Lee Heidenblut (Finalist and Honorable Mention)

Looking down at the piece of paper with unbroken concentration, he guided his steady hand across the page to form a perfect circle, to which he added four lines. Brady smiled when he drew the last line. To him, it was perfect and he considered it a work of art that could rival all those fancy paintings in the museum. He stood up from the base of the couch, where he had previously lain, and showed the picture to his mom. She sat with her legs crossed on the couch right behind him and watched the news with the same funny face she had whenever Brady's saw his daddy on tv. Just a few months ago, Brady came down the stairs and his mommy was watching the tv, just like she was now, with that look. Brady remembered his mommy had told him that it was a real live bank robbery and his daddy was one of the police officers that went to help.

The look his mommy had on her face made Brady feel a little sad, because she looked sad. But even Brady's six year old mind could tell that, in her eyes, there was something more than just sadness. She looked scared. Brady didn't know why because, granted he was a police officer, nothing could happen to his dad. He was Brady's hero and best friend. Brady thought he was invincible, just like the superheroes in his comics. But every time Brady saw his dad on tv, him mommy always had that sad, scared look on her face and he just didn't know why.

It took a little while for Brady to get his mommy's attention. Each time he said her name, he assumed that the tv was too loud and she just couldn't hear him. So he said it again and again, "Mommy...Mommy? Mom. Hey Mommy," until it finally got her attention.

She managed to take her eyes away, but just for a moment because something caught her attention again and she forgot. She was back to watching the tv. "Mommy, you didn't look." She was awful distracted today. She had been making dinner and right in the middle of dishing it out for Brady, she had wandered away and started to watch tv. But that was OK, Brady just got a stool and got it himself. She could be so silly sometime, thought Brady lovingly. She took her eyes away this time long enough so really look at the picture of his father in his blue uniform. His mother, who seemed to be on autopilot, gave him a small smile and a kiss on the cheek. Then her smile was gone and she went back to watching the tv. Since the tv was so interesting to her, Brady decided to give it a chance and watched just like she did. His crystal blue eyes stared at the screen that flashed between shots of a burning building and pictures of firefighters dosing every flame that dared show itself through the shattered windows.

Brady's mommy chewed her finger and said something coming out. "What?" asked Brady thinking she was talking to him.

"Nothing honey." Brady kept watching even though it was boring.

After what seemed like an eternity of watching the boring news, Brady quietly said to his mother, "This is boring. Can we watch something else?" to which she didn't respond. Suddenly, the newscasters began talking and there was excitement in their voices. The camera zoomed in on a figure wearing blue clothes and carrying a child, not much younger than Brady. As they emerged from the billowing smoke, recognition lit Brady's face as he realized the person on the tv was none other than his very own daddy. Brady thought it would be helpful to let his mom know that it was his daddy since she was so distracted today. "Hey mommy look, that's daddy! He just saved the boy! Isn't he brave?" Again, she didn't say anything and Brady found this very irritating. So, to fill the silence, he said to himself, "I hope someday I'm as brave as daddy."

Brady loved it when he got to stay up to wait for his daddy to come home but it was always a long time so he waited in his room where he could play with his toys. He wanted to practice being brave so he found the biggest stuffed animal he could find in his hoard of plush toys. It happened to be a light brown lion with a huge, soft mane and open jaws showing terrifying, fabric jaws. Brady pictured the lion roaring at him so he thought it proper to roar back. Then, with one, explosive leap, he jumped on the stuffed animal and wrestled it to the ground. It would be silly to wrestle something that didn't fight back every so often, so Brady occasionally gave the lion a little help and guided its claws across his own chest, pretended to be hurt but still be strong enough to fight back.

He kept this charade up until the voice of his father spoke from the doorway. "Careful Brady! Don't let it bite you!" Brady looked up from his enemy and saw his father leaning against the doorframe. He rushed over and buried himself in his father's crispy, cold uniform. New York was cold this time of year.

Brady always loved hugging his dad. Whenever he was sad or scared, all he needed to do was hug his dad, to bury his face in his uniform, and all the fear and sadness would melt away.

"Daddy! I saw you save that boy on tv! You're so brave." Brady looked up at him as he said this so he could marvel at his dad. Brady found he was so excited for his father that he jumped up and down.

His dad coughed from inhaling the smoke but then he kneeled down so he was eye to eye with his son. "And I should have waited for the firefighters. If something had happened to me, you wouldn't have a father... and I'm so sorry," he paused and looked behind him in the dark hallway where Brady's mom was standing. "You know who the brave one is? Your mom. Even though it scares her, she lets me do what I love."

Brady was excited to hear that his mom was brave, too. Recently, it had been Brady's life's goal to catch a frog at the pond in Central Park but now he wanted nothing more than to be brave like his parents. He told his father, "Well, I'm brave just like you and mommy! I just beat up my pet lion, oh, but he's alright." He pointed his small finger at the plush lion sprawled on the floor.

"And you are brave, son. But beating a lion doesn't make you courage, it makes you strong. What does take courage is when you do something that scares you," said his father. He stood up and turned out the light. "Now, if you and the lion can still stand each other, I want you two to hop in bed and go to sleep. You have school tomorrow."

Brady frowned. He didn't like school that much and not to mention there was a big kid named Leo who pushed everyone around. Brady thought about the bully as his parents helped him into bed. Last time he had seen Leo, the bully told him if he didn't give him a dollar, he would punch him. Usually, the bully rode the bus that picked Brady up so he resolved to get up early and walk to school.

———

That night he dreamt only of punching the bully until he cried like a baby. He dreamt he did it on the bus. He dreamt he did it at school in the cafeteria and on the playground. Then when he was walking home from school in his dream, the bully jumped out of the bushes and tackled him but Brady still fought him off. Brady wasn't sure how he did it but it was just a dream so why would he care?

But then the dream turned sour. His father was hugging him and telling him how brave he was for fighting the bully when out of nowhere, the bully grabbed him and kicked him, punched him, beat him until he couldn't get up. All the meanwhile his father was standing over them yelling at Brady to get up but Brady just couldn't. When things couldn't get any worse, the bully began growing and growing until he was bigger than the house and his head broke through the ceiling. But he just kept growing until Brady couldn't see his face anymore, just his body. Pinned down under the massive foot, Brady watched as Leo began growing faster until he was bigger than the big buildings down the street! Then with two fingers bigger than trucks, Leo the bully picked Brady up and threw him out of the town saying, "you'll never be brave like your father if you can't fight me!" Brady was flying through the air crying, weeping. He was going to hit the ground and hard. He closed his eyes, cried out and waited for it to happen.

When he was just millimeters from hitting the ground, everything stopped and Brady could feel warm strong arms around him. Opening his eyes to the real world, he saw his father looking down at him. Brady whimpered a little.

Repeating it over and over, his father told him he was ok and the dream was over. "You want to tell me about it?" he finally said.

Brady nodded but didn't say anything for a while. He was too scared it would come true if he said it out loud. Then Brady complied, "I was being brave and I was fighting Leo the bully. Then I came home and you were telling me I was brave but then he came and beat me up." Brady whimpered again. "Then he grew so big he picked me up and threw me away and told me I would never be brave like you are, Daddy...and...and..."

Brady's father didn't even let Brady finish before he said, "Oh, son. Remember what I said? Courage isn't being strong enough to fight a bully, it's being brave enough to stand up to him. It's being brave enough to tell him that you aren't afraid of him and that he can't bully you anymore, even though it scares you. Anyone can throw a punch to fight someone but not everyone can stand up to someone and be brave enough to not throw a punch. And just getting hit doesn't make you a coward. If anything, it makes you braver because you're not running away. Don't you see?"

Brady was embarrassed that he had forgotten what his dad said. He was so preoccupied with wanting to be brave like his parents, he hadn't listened to his dad when he told him what bravery was. He wondered if he would ever be brave so he asked, who knew everything, "Daddy, what do I do to be brave like you?"

Brady's daddy looked him in the eyes, "All you have to do, is do something, even though you're scared. That's all it takes, son."

———————

Brady grabbed extra money this time. It wouldn't hurt to rub it in that he had more than a dollar when he refused to give Leo his money. He stuffed his pockets full of quarters, dimes, nickels and any other object that resembled a coin. He was determined that today, none of it would go home with Leo. Excited to prove himself brave today, he ate faster than he should have and got the hiccups for a little while. His dad had already left for work so Brady didn't get the chance to tell him that he was going to be brave today and stand up to Leo.

Brady had it all planned out. He was going to pull out the money, wave it in Leo's face and then stuff it in his pocket and tell him that he was never going to take his money again. It scared him but when he did it, then he knew he'd be brave. He would stand his ground though he possessed no power over Leo.

Walking out the door with his backpack and lunchbox, Brady was so excited, he ran to the bus stop and his mommy could barely keep up. He got on the bus and looked to the back where Leo usually sat. Brady was actually a little disappointed to see that Leo wasn't sitting there. He must have walked to school.

Leo wasn't at his locker either. Brady was ten lockers down and Leo was almost always at his locker when he wasn't bullying kids into giving him money.

During recess, Brady ran to the playground and climbed to the top of the play structure. From his vantage point, he could see most of the school. His eyes scanned over each kid running around looking for the bulky sixth grader he longed to see. But he wasn't there. He did see, however, Mrs. Sache, the sixth-grade teacher. Brady ran up to her and asked where Leo was.

She called after one of the children to stop tugging another kid's hair then replied, "he got expelled for stealing the bake sale's money and framing it on one of the other kids."

Dejected, Brady walked away. Now he didn't have the chance to stand up to Leo. Class went by slowly and dully until the lunch bell rang. Even then, amongst all the kids laughing and happy to be one lunch break, Brady was frowning and his neck hung low.

By the time the school day was over, he was feeling terrible. He hadn't gotten a chance to stand up to Leo. Brady figured the best way to cheer up was to find his best friend, Nick, who was in second grade. Nick and Brady usually sat by the flagpole when they waited for their parents to pick them up.

Brady spotted Nick next to their spot. He called out but over the chatter of dozens of kids, it was no wonder why Nick didn't hear him. Plus, he was talking to another boy. But as Brady got closer, he saw that the boy Nick was talking to was actually holding Nick by the collar and holding a fist to Nick's nose. The boy was at least three grades ahead of Brady and three inches taller. This was not the kind of boy that Brady wanted to mess with. He would end up with a loose tooth or black eye if he messed with this kid.

His feet started moving in the other direction but after a few steps, he stopped. He was scared, wasn't he? That's why he was walking away, wasn't it? Brady's feet turned around now. Confidently, he strode with clenched fists and kicked the new bully's shoes. "Stop it! Let him go!" yelled Brady staring him down.

Turning around to face the newcomer, the new kid sized up Brady and laughed when he saw the small, first grader looking at him in the eye. "Get lost unless you want a punch in the nose," said the new kid.

Brady thought of some quip to say back. "How about you get lost or maybe you'll be the one with a bloody nose." Brady liked that. It made him sound tough. Nick was wide-eyed when he saw Brady, of all people, standing up to this bully. Brady wanted to run, but because his daddy said that it took even more courage to not run away, he didn't budge. The bully raised his fist to punch Brady in the mouth. But Brady smiled, thinking what his daddy would think when he told him about this.

The smile did not go unnoticed by the bully. It was unusual for such a small kid to be smiling in a situation like this. He let go of Nick and looked around. And walked away.

Brady and Nick were stunned. This had never happened to them before and they didn't know if it was going to keep happening or not. Finally, Nick said, "Wow, thanks Brady, he was gunna take my lunch money! But oh, saw your dad over there earlier!"

Brady turned and looked where Nick pointed. By the looks of it, his daddy had been there for a while. He leaned against his police car in his sharp winter uniform and smiled like he usually did when he picked Brady up. But his smile was different and Brady knew his daddy had seen what went on. He also guessed that his daddy's gaze was what scared the bully off and kept him from getting punched. But it didn't matter whether Brady got punched or not. He had stood his ground just like his daddy said he should and that was what mattered. In just that one smile, Brady's father expressed all pride and joy a father could ever feel for a son.

What Does It Feel Like To Be a Teenager?

By Paysen Hudson (Finalist)

What does it feel like to be a teenager? It's the feeling of having the time of your life while also having the worst time of your life. Confusing? So is being a teenager. We are suddenly thrown into being somewhere in between a kid and an adult. You don't really feel like a teen until you are sixteen when you can drive. And TV shows and movies have installed impossible expectations in me. But there are moments when it all comes together, and you feel like you are in those exact videos. When you are diving and jamming out to your favorite song with the windows down, you feel like a stereotypical teen. But it doesn't matter, because you feel like you are on top of the world. Or you are sitting down, maybe contemplating something or just studying. Suddenly, you are a teen at a critical point in a movie or TV show.

But there is also the fear of the future. I mean, you are in school competing for a grade and a spot in a "good" college or university. It can be the worst. And it only keeps getting worse for teens. The school system hasn't changed much in the one hundred years it's been in use. It was made for children to learn to work in a factory, so now that isn't an option, shouldn't they have changed it? They put hundreds of kids together in a school and put the same standard on all. As a country, I thought we would have improved at least a little. We have learned from some of the most successful inventors that education wasn't reliant on them going to school but from their own creativity and learning from others.

When a school puts a standard on everyone, they shouldn't expect everyone to meet it. Some people aren't meant for the standards of the specific subjects but are brilliant in their own way. Having a number given telling you how smart you are is demeaning. Telling someone they are dumb in a specific subject or, an adult's personal favorite, you are lazy. Sometimes it's just hard to have all this work that doesn't help at all and still keep the recommended amount of sleep and activity is too tiring. We have large expectations placed on us.

And the constant, "In my day..." is completely unnecessary. We understand times were different or simpler, but we would prefer to stay in our time with our technology we use as an escape. Life can sometimes be too much, so we spend some of it on our devices. It doesn't always mean we are obsessed; it just means we are struggling and have already had too much social interaction. Being a teenager presents a whole new load of challenges we all struggle with. It is no help to hear adults tell us we are the worst and the hardest. We know we are the hardest because we are trying our hardest. Just take a deep breath, and please have patience with us. We try and we have to make some mistakes, but we mostly mean good. We just want these last years of freedom from responsibility to be fun and full of everything we have ever wanted. We don't always make the best choices or even think about the consequences. Sometimes we don't care about what you have to say or what is happening around us. It's overwhelming and trying on all of us, I promise. So, what does it feel like to be a teenager? It's feeling like you rule the world while also feeling like you are the worst part of the world. We have many conflicting emotions, and you can't always figure us out. But we are the future and we are amazing!

How I Grew to Love my Culture

By Melanie Antony (Finalist)

I am the daughter of immigrants, and my parents sacrificed everything to come to this country. I am so proud to be an Indian-American, and my culture has always been a big part of my life. However, my entire life I have always felt out of place. Being the child of immigrants and trying to balance both sides of my life. It's a constant identity struggle. I live in a primarily white town, and growing up have experienced a lot of racism. I specifically remember being told I couldn't play with a group of kids because I was brown. In another instance, in middle school, a group of boys found it funny to tease me about being Indian, and they nicknamed me "curry girl". They told me I smelled and would drench my locker with cologne and ridicule me in the hallways. I tried to fit in more by buying my lunch instead of bringing fragrant Indian food. Around this time, my grandma came to live with us from India. She would always cook these intricate Indian dishes. She spoke a little English, but her way of showing her love was through her food, not words. Her dishes were packed with flavor, and most importantly her love. My grandma would spend hours cooking and I would watch her in awe from the kitchen table. I would help her out by grating coconut or cutting vegetables and would be so excited to eat the delicious food she prepared. When my grandma passed away the following year, I was heartbroken. I was able to find a way to honor her memory, and was able to do that through cooking her old dishes. I have always had a passion for science, and I realized that cooking food is like an experiment. The recipe is the procedure, and you need to measure everything out for it to work. The flavor proportions are scientific, and various chemical reactions take place when you are cooking. I remember my first time making my grandma's signature chicken curry. The recipe was daunting with many steps and ingredients. I took on the challenge and got to work. My mom helped me find the spices I needed, and I remember the aroma that filled the air when I fried the spices. This was the aroma that smelled so delicious to me, yet also smelled disgusting to my peers. I approached curry as a science experiment, and delicious marriage of an assortment of spices, whereas the kids at school saw it as gross and weird looking. I realized that these kids were brought up in a different way than I had, and my culture was something that made me unique, not weird. I struggled growing up in two worlds, but now, I appreciate my unique cultural perspective and being been born into such a beautiful culture with delicious food.

Broken

By Ava Robinson (Finalist)

"People can't come back to life."

My neighbor had said it. It was the only comment from the funeral I remembered. It was so rude; like someone was stabbing me with a red-hot spike. I could feel the guilt, the pain. I knew she missed him, but it wasn't my fault.

It wasn't my fault. The words echoed through my brain, laughing with demonic glee.

I was the one who told him to stay home, wasn't I?

It was me who told him that I could do it on my own; he'd only get hurt. So why was it my fault?

I didn't stop him. He still followed me and I led him to his death. But I told him not to. I squeezed my eyes shut, but it only made the nightmare clearer.

"I can't let you go alone," I heard his voice, gentle and coaxing. "You could get hurt, Jina. You could die."

His eyes were so soft, so precious. They looked up at me in devotion and trust. I failed him.

I felt a tear burn my cheek as I remembered his eyes when he died. They were full of pain and love.

"It's not your fault, Jina."

Those had been his last words. I didn't believe them. It had been my mission, not his. He didn't even know how to fight, or fire a Glock. My little brother, fresh from high school, wanting to join the army like I had. Wanting to follow in his idolized big sister's footsteps. Wanting to be a hero. He was like that, always wanting to help. Right up until the end.

I opened my eyes quickly; I didn't want to rerun what happened next. I felt the hot tears roll down to my chin. I saw it all play out.

He had wanted to help me. I caved in and let him come. I thought it would be safe. The mission was going smoothly; he had stood rigidly beside me as the transactions were going through. I was invisible to the security system. I always was. But he wasn't. I remembered the look on his face as the alarm wailed and flashed and as the guards raised their guns. Panic and trust. Blind trust.

I took out the guards; it didn't take long. Then it happened. The shot rang out, deafening. So loud it was silent. I felt like a spectator, like I was just watching. I could see the bullet streaking towards me, like in the movies; slow motion. But I couldn't move. I was glued to the ground. The bullet moving so fast it was frozen in time.

He could move. And he did. He leapt; I hadn't known he could move so fast, faster than the bullet. He caught the bullet for me.

I wiped the tears that had gathered at my chin.

I remembered the horror. The blood bubbling from his chest and dripping from the corner of his mouth.

Scarlet life trickling away.

I killed the guard.

He took my brother.

It was his fault.

I opened my eyes again and stared at the picture next to the greeting table. His smile. It was so full, I could feel his soul grinning. I remembered when he first found out who I had become. That same grin, "You mean my sister is a spy?" His eyes twinkling and brown hair waving in the breeze, "You're so cool, Jina."

I didn't find it cool that that's what killed him. He was like no other sibling I knew. He said the same about me, but that was because of my job, not my character.

He was so young; it should have been me under the flag. It should have been me with the flowers cascading over the lid and the slideshow of random selfies he took of us together.

There was nothing left for me here. He was all I had.

No one came to console me. No one knew exactly how he had died. The story was about a car crash. I couldn't remember all the details they had wanted me to say. I had told the car crash story before, but it was at other funerals with mourners I didn't know. They said that it would be the same. But it wasn't. Not when it was my brother in the ground.

I pushed through the doors and slid into my car. My hands fumbled with the keys. Driving away hurt. Flashes of his life, his smile ... his blood filled my mind. Those last words.

It was all my fault. No one else's.

I drove on. I left it all behind. The picture of us together on the beach after our parents' funeral flapped on the dashboard.

I'd arrive in some small town, and say I'd gotten lost. I'd be invisible. I was good at that. I'd run from my past, not forgetting, but just letting go.

I'd start again. But could I without him?

I'd have to. There weren't any strong arms to fall back into or warm smiles to be supported by. It was just me. I was all alone.

"People can't come back to life."

Maybe not. He was gone for good. But I could die to the world and come back as someone else.

I let the miles swallow me. I didn't care where I went, as long as it wasn't back to that hollow house where we'd stay up on summer nights and stargaze. Where he'd make up constellations and tell me fantastic stories about them. Where we'd laugh.

I'd be called in for another op, I knew it. They wouldn't care. But I could just forget to pick up the phone. They'd find me eventually, but it would take a little while. I was betting on that. After all, they'd turned me into a ghost, and a shadow, hadn't they? I could maybe, just for a while, be normal. Maybe I'd be able to forget the pain. And I could grieve.

Creux

By Carolina Herrera (Finalist)

The sound of a dozen keys jangling breaks an eerie silence as Ana struggles to unlock the back door of her restaurant.

It's 5 in the morning and the rest of Chicago is still fast asleep. Ana has been working as the head chef and owner of Creux, a high-end French restaurant, for almost five years now. Her crisp chef's coat is peeking out under the three layers of jackets she had put on at home in a failed attempt to stay warm.

A sudden whine and rustle somewhere in the restaurant's dumpster interrupts her focus. With sunken eyes and jagged movements, Ana pauses to investigate. Not finding anything out of the ordinary she instead makes a mental note to take out the trash before returning to the task at hand. A sigh and a shiver later she finds the right key and enters Creux.

It's obvious she's one for routine.

Ana makes her way around the stainless steel kitchen in a well-practiced dance. First, each of her jackets take up their own hanger to the right of the entrance. She makes sure to smooth out any wrinkles on them before heading to turn on every light. The ceiling lights are cold and harsh, unforgiving in how they highlight the sharpness of her cheekbones and the sparsity of her hair. Next she takes inventory. Ana's records of the pantry and fridge are meticulous. She registers that they are running low on bread and swiftly highlights the note in blue. She closes the fridge and regards the stranger in her reflection on the door's spotless surface. With the same monotony and disinterest, Ana lifts her chef's coat to check how her ribs protrude and takes an odd comfort in doing so.

As the first streaks of daylight break through, Ana is washing vegetables at the sink facing a small window that shows the alleyway behind the kitchen. Her head spins just at the thought of the work that lies ahead. The microwave hums quietly behind her as it heats up a sugar-less, milk-less coffee. A brie and cucumber sandwich sits next to the microwave patiently.

The first rays of light leak into the kitchen and Ana begins to feel warm. This sensation triggers memories of enjoying the sun with family on weekly picnics back when she would bake new French pastries for them to try. If it wasn't for them, Ana would have never had the confidence to open up her own restaurant. She started Creux as an extension of her passion for caring for others and just five years later she stands as one of the most accomplished young female chefs in the nation. A humble smile plays weakly across her face as she reminisces.

The microwave beeps just as Ana finishes prepping and washing the day's ingredients. She looks up and out the window to decide if the weather would allow for breakfast outside.

Two begging eyes meet her gaze. A small, shivering beagle is sitting in the alley with trash strewn around it.

The sun is now up and the alleyway looks more inviting than it did in the dark. Layered up once again, Ana slips out the back door with her coffee and sandwich in hand. She takes a seat on the curb and the beagle approaches her, whining.

Judging from its size Ana reckons the dog is only a puppy, but the darkness around its eyes lets her know it has been through a lot more than its age lets on. The puppy's pronounced ribs seem foreign to her; she wonders why any creature should have to suffer like that.

A chuckle escapes Ana's mouth as she realizes the twisted irony of her situation. The beagle tilts its head in an attempt to understand. Glancing back and forth between the dumpster and the puppy, Ana decides not to throw away her breakfast like she would any other morning.

With a humph of anxious determination, she splits the sandwich in half and sets part of it down for the dog.

She takes a mental note to double the next order of brie cheese and then bites her sandwich. Sounds of the city's traffic rise around them as Ana finally truly feels the warmth she has only ever allowed herself to give away.

Homeless

By Lakyn Russell (Finalist)

Everyday is an endless search when you're homeless. A fight for my own survival. I have had to learn to look out for myself. Through the severely bitter and frigid winters that freeze the tips of my ears down to my pinky toes. Through the scorching hot summers that melt my skin to the pavement. Through the bee stings and the allergies that spring brings. Through the colorless rainy days of fall when everything dies. Everyday I take the scraps of what other people are willing to give. Mostly the leftover change they have after they bought their morning coffee. Or a crumpled five dollar bill they happened to have in their big brown leather wallets. The leftovers are better than nothing. I have learned to take what life gives you. Or in this case what some stranger on the street has just enough of to give a little bit to you.

I don't mind being homeless though. It's like being invisible, which is like having a superpower. You can stand right in front of people but they won't see you. You can be sitting on the side of the road in a field amongst the weeds and people will only look at the wild flowers that grow next to you. If I think about it like this then I can pretend that it doesn't hurt when people quickly turn away after accidentally making eye contact. Or when they give you a sorry smile before going on about their day. What hurts the most is when they try to get rid of you. Like my life is a disturbance. Like my presence is an inconvenience to people who have a home. They don't want to see me in front of their grocery store when they just need to get bread. They don't want to see me when they have come to a stop at a red light. They don't want to see me when they walk down the street. They don't want to see me.

Today, as I sat along the concrete sidewalk, I noticed an older man, who like me was alone. His warm brown eyes stared at me intently. I began to feel uncomfortable. He started to make his way over and I noticed a soft smile creep into the corners of his mouth. "Hello." He said simply. His voice was gentle and soft. "What is your name?" He asked.

We spent some time going through introductions. I told him everything I knew about myself. I don't why but it felt like I was waiting my whole life for somebody to ask. He looked at me like we were the same. Unlike others who separated themselves from me, forgetting that I was in fact one of them. When he talked to me he didn't talk down to me like I was less than him. He sat down right in front of me. He didn't hover above or look down on me. He looked me directly in the eyes and talked to me. He didn't hand me cash or food, he just talked to me.

"Why are you homeless?" he asked finally, I could tell it was the question he was most curious about. His eyes were wide in anticipation for my response.

I lowered my head and replied, "What's so good about having a home? I learned a long time ago to take what life gives you." He nodded his head as if that was what he expected to hear.

"I was once homeless." He said matter of factly. "I used to think the same way. Until someone came and offered me an opportunity. Then I learned why people work so hard to have a home."

"Why?" I asked, desperately like it was the answer I had been waiting to hear my whole life.

"Because a home is not only a place you have to return to. A home protects you from every bitter winter and scorching hot summer. A home is where you can watch the flowers bloom in the springtime and the leaves turn colors during the fall. A home can protect you from all the seasons." He smiled softly.

The Decision that Changed my Life

By Steve Samson (Finalist)

Before my eyes stood the very decision that would change my life. A decision that would lead to the promised land or the very depths of hell. My hand struggled to put the pen to the paper. The man with the black suit cleared his throat. "Come on, Mr. Brown," he said with a sinister grin. "It'll be the best decision of your life." He rubbed his hands like he was creating a fire from the air.

As he sat there, he thought about yesterday. The studio was full of life. To no one's surprise, Jonathan Brown had made something magical. Music so majestic, with so many intricate sounds, it could've topped the Billboards. At this point, they were just having fun. "Look what we've made here," said Jonathan.

"You really know how to work magic, man," said Derrick.

"That's what he does," said Jeffrey, Jonathan's brother.

"I appreciate y'all," said Jonathan, "It means a lot. I finally got something to put up online."

"You know," Derrick said, "you could make a lot more money off of this. You just need a record deal."

"Yeah, when are you getting signed?" Jeffrey asked optimistically.

"I didn't know when to tell you this," said Jonathan, "But I got an offer."

"What?" said Derrick, "That's amazing!"

"When are you accepting it?" asked Jeffrey.

"I don't know if I will," Jonathan replied hesitantly, "It's a lot."

"Why not?" Jeffrey was enraged. "You don't like money?"

"Do you think this is easy? I don't want to sell my soul for a company. I got a wife and 2 kids at home! I gotta be there for them."

"I'm sure they could use the money too," Derrick said while trying to calm everyone down.

"I know," Jonathan said, "I know. But I don't know what to do. All I know is that I gotta make my decision tomorrow."

I packed up my gear and went out. I went to the one place where I could get answers. The place that I hadn't been in for over a year. I knocked on the door with what sounded like defeat. Out came my mother. She was I surprised as I was. She was looking back at me was the same somber face I was making. She let me in.

It started off with the usual. Why had I chosen this lifestyle? Didn't I hear her say I shouldn't? How do you plan on supporting your family? These were all questions that I never stopped getting when I decided to make music. These questions seemed to multiply when dad died. He had put his soul into his music. She said that's what killed him, even when the doctors told her it was a heart attack.

"So you're telling me that you got an offer for some record company. Do you know what happened to your father?" she asked me.

"Mama, it was a heart attack," I replied.

"What do you think caused it? Do you think a healthy man in his 40s would just die of a heart attack just like that with no warning?" She stared at me but I couldn't return the look.

"Mama, this is the biggest deal of my life. I could finally make it."

"Is that what's important to you. Making it? That's the same ambition your father once had. He poured nights in that studio. Nights without me or you or your brother. And where did that take him? " I sat in uncomfortable silence.

"Mama..." I started to say.

"You're going to listen to me. You can't come into my house thinking about yourself and 'making it'. You have a family at home. I know they could use the money. But they need their father"

And with that, she told me to leave her house and make the right decision.

I sat there inside the studio of Hot Records. The contract was there. I had read it over so many times I had practically memorized it. In big bold print, clear as day, was a number. A number followed by 6 zeros. This was my opportunity. But looking at the schedule, the tours, and the sessions, there was no time to be a father. I thought back to what my mother said.

"Well?" asked Mr. Dreamer, the owner of Hot Records, "Go ahead, Mr. Brown. Sign it. You won't regret it." He continued to rub his hands with that same sinister smile.

I looked at him and with a determined look and I whispered the word "No". He asked me to repeat myself. And I said it louder.

"No. I can't do it." My hand stopped shaking and I put the pen down with authority. I packed my things. "I have to see my kids man. I need to be a father. They're worth more than any contract you'll give me."

As I headed out the door, I could hear him say, "Wait! You're making a mistake!" But there was no turning back.

The devil himself stood there in disappointment. No one had ever turned down his offer. Not even Jonathan's father could resist. It was one less soul to claim for himself. For the first time, he failed.

The Forbidden Marshmallows

By Abdul Cherchar (Finalist)

As my friends and I waited for dessert, the sweet, inviting smell of the chocolate was intoxicating; I kept my eye on the dessert plate as I waited for my own order. The smell of the chocolate kept me distracted and thrilled while waiting for my order. Once my own dessert came, I ate non-stop. Even though I was finished and felt full, I accepted a piece of dessert my friend offered from his own; I never realized exactly what I was eating! All I know is that it was delightful; I could not get enough of it; it was a rich, sugary, puffy, roasted confection, coated with milk chocolate. I love sweets and I could not believe that I had never been introduced to this pillow of goodness before. "What was that?" I asked. "Milk chocolate with marshmallows," he said. I felt a shock running through my spine. I did not say a word afterward? Once I realized I had eaten marshmallows, my

mental state buzzed with anxiety. I left the restaurant and headed straight home! The thought of my sin consumed me; as a practicing Muslim, I am not allowed to ever eat pork and the gelatin in marshmallows is pork derivative. I felt like I'd betrayed my religion and my family. I had broken my promise to my religion and I also felt that I could not tell my parents for fear of disappointing them. Despite feeling all this guilt, I still thought about the marshmallow treat! I realized that my situation was worse than I originally thought. I would need to resolve the problem immediately; I was troubled with it for the rest of the day and it has kept me up for the entire night! By the following morning, I came to the decision to repent and pretend that nothing had happened.

Afterward, I went to the mosque where I prayed to Allah, in other words, god, and repented for one hour. After I left, I felt like all my bad actions had been diminished. Because I felt this way, I believed that I wouldn't eat marshmallows again. However, my conclusion proved to be wrong. The following weekend, my friend invited me to go out and eat dessert again. When we ate dessert, my friend ordered s'mores again! This time I was jealous because the s'mores looked delicious. I did not want to think about it, but my inner- self was telling me to eat it! At that moment, my desire for marshmallows surpassed the promise I had made. I asked him for a piece of s'mores and ate without thinking of my actions again. This time, something was really wrong. I didn't feel as guilty as I had before, and I quickly realized that this was a serious problem. I decided that I absolutely needed to come to terms with my actions and of course reevaluate how I felt about my decisions. The next day, I made a final plan to end this conflict. I said to myself that if I thought about marshmallows, I would pray each time. As time passed, I continuously followed this plan and struggled.

However, I ultimately made a huge success with my plan on my own.

Struggling over a desire was challenging, but what I learned from this setback was self-control and the technique of replacement for gaining it. Having self-control as a student has made many aspects of my life much easier—relationships, academics, and extra pursuits. I can regulate my actions which can prevent me from doing inappropriate things. Though being a Muslim in modern times is tough, the struggles I've accepted as a result have enabled me to learn to manage my needs independently and exercise control when things get tough. Overall, this experience allowed me to become much more controlled as an individual and become more committed and dedicated to my beliefs.

Puzzle Pieces

By Prapthi Jayesh Sirrkay (Finalist)

Sprawled out on the lavish brown couch in my living room, I study the birds that nibble on the food from the rusty red feeder, suspended off a tree in my wooded backyard. I am reminded of my journey of over 8,500 miles from my home in India to my modest apartment in Eagan.

My mom fries onions for our traditional Indian dinner in the kitchen and the aroma wafts through the house. When I was younger, the smell was bothersome. The rich flavors of authentic Indian food would carry on my backpack, my lunch bag, and the strong smell of roasted spices would float through the halls. The odor would not only linger on my clothes but would trail into the lunchroom as soon as I opened my maroon Tupperware lunch box. The smell that once delighted me in India and turned to a stench that caused embarrassment. Most people just stared at me, and others got curious as I would break apart my naan in a practiced way with my bare hands.

""Ew, what is that?""

""You just eat that with your hands?""

Their words did not cut, so much as they make me nauseous. Growing up as part of two cultures, I was often conflicted as to which one I identified with more. A cloud of discomfort surrounded me. There I sat like a deer in headlights, stunned at the comments of my classmates. There I sat, peerless and awkward. The looks continued for days until the appetizing taste of my naan turned to a bland one. I realized it would be less humiliating to throw my naan into the trash cans instead of feeling the weight of my peers' eyes. I used to enjoy dipping my fresh naan into aromatic paneer masala, but I no longer could without the stares of my peers.

I am a horrible person. There are people in the world that are starving. However, the damage was done. I no longer had the stomach for my mother's Indian food. The hurtful words of my peers not only led me to feel embarrassed but also invoked a sense of destitution that led me to believe it would be better not to open my lunch at all.

Suppressing my love for Indian food was one of the first steps that I took to assimilate. Twig by twig, I was building a new nest in an unfamiliar place. My distinct Indian accent changed into a more modern Minnesotan one. My connections with my friends from India followed soon after. Like the rope in a game of Tug of War, I grappled between trying to fit in and remembering my identity. I was ashamed of my culture.

Biennially, I visit my hometown of Bangalore. I stepped out of the Bangalore airport, and as soon as I left the air-conditioned building, the sweltering heat encompassed my body. Instantly, I felt isolated in a crowd of my people. Naturally, I should have felt at home, but I did not. I had assimilated. I was an outcast.

I am no longer part of the culture that I was born into, but I am not part of another. The looks from passersby are subtle, but I see them. My accent is thick but not the same as it used to be. The Indian slang I once understood now sounds alien. I am no longer a person that watches cricket every Sunday. Yet, I am still not the person that watches the football game between the Packers and Vikings. I don't conform to the social norms of Indian culture, yet I do not satisfy the conditions to be a true American.

A part of me has changed. A feeling of ego and arrogance floods me as I am aware of the privileged life I have led in America. Having an American accent warrants a sense of pride. In an attempt to fit in, I act entitled. In a powerful voice, I speak in English to my mother, almost as a child boasting about a new toy. I make my presence known. In India, everyone envies those who live in America. The paradoxical part is that I am just as Indian as I am American.

The night before my cousin Diya's birthday party, our distant and close families gather at their home in Bangalore. A group of distant relatives all visit with their sons and daughters. They sit around the spacious living room, and the adults make conversation. Bollywood pop songs blast through the TV as the group rejoices about her recent academic feats. The teens tease her, and the adults laugh along. Their faces gleam with a sense of contentment. There is nowhere they would rather be at this moment. They radiate optimism and positivity, yet their laughter turns to a cackle in my head. The warm air surrounds me, yet a sense of solitude settled in. It is almost ironic how well everyone knew each other. The moment is fleeting, and I would rather be anywhere other than here. Perhaps, I don't want to fit in. Perhaps, I do not know how to. They fit together in perfect harmony, a box of puzzle pieces.

I sit in the corner and watch from afar. Their jokes fly over my head. Their language, one that I am fluent in, seems foreign. I am no longer part of this puzzle. I am an outsider.

My name is Prapthi Jayesh Sirkay. I hold a name that is Indian, yet I have spent over fourteen years of my life in countries where the national language is English. I have heard a variation of pronunciations of my name, Prap-uh-they, Prop-that, and Prop-tee. Despite the embarrassment it caused growing up, I have found a certain sense of appreciation for my name.

I am an outsider to both worlds. I am a part of both, and I am a part of neither. I am both the missing puzzle piece and the outcast.

My Aspergian Arch-Nemesis

By Ian Cann (Finalist)

During my childhood, I became aware that I had an arch-nemesis. Early on, I knew that library books brought me more joy than recess games and making friends was more difficult for me than others. As I grew older, my nemesis lurked within me. My social anxiety loomed as I saw how my way of interpreting the world was different. This was perplexing until a few years ago when my nemesis was revealed: I was diagnosed with Asperger Syndrome.

Aspergers brings a fair share of challenges. Deciphering normal social cues can be taxing, but I have devised strategies for dealing with the anxiety this produces. I've found that I struggle to perform everyday tasks when I have to synthesize multiple needs while simultaneously responding in a socially appropriate way. I have learned to decode my own nuances while unveiling the workings of the neurotypical world. Essentially, becoming a detective of human behavior helped quelch the anxiety Aspergers has wrought in me.

While I still struggle with communicating at times, I learned to use common interests, humor, and honesty in my interactions. Aspergers can easily create a barrier to friendships since it requires more effort and time to develop friendships with Aspergers. I learn from my social missteps and am fortunate that my parents and friends are willing to help me navigate social situations.

However, though my enemy throws obstacles in my path, I've found unintended benefits. And, like any good arch-enemy, dealing with mine has revealed my superpower: determination. I love to learn and fully immerse myself in school projects and hobbies. Admittedly, while I am not naturally gifted in certain areas, I do always work hard to overcome obstacles when I struggle. My determination and focus push me to constantly improve myself and not capitulate when faced with a barrier. This is especially important with my anxiety and the challenges I face with communication; it is my determination to be engaged that motivates me to pursue friendships and involvement in activities.

I have come to make peace with my nemesis. For, we are one in the same. Instead of seeing the limitations from having Aspergers, I see the opportunity for growth. I couldn't have faced these difficulties on my own and I have benefited from the support of my community. It may not be readily apparent to my classmates or teachers that I have Aspergers, but my experiences have shown me that not all our challenges are readily seen. I really appreciate the ways my Aspergers has expanded my understanding of myself and others.

Now, I pay it forward and look for opportunities to be an advocate for people who have villains of their own. I just hope that there isn't a surprise "post-credits scene" that foreshadows the next villain of my life! But even if there is, I know that with my determination and grit I'll be able to defeat them, and hopefully uncover a positive outcome from their evil scheme.

Narcissus

By Diana Song (Finalist)

In big, bold lettering on a billboard: CALL TODAY FOR HAPPINESS.

"Was your day really that bad?" His father looks back from the wheel and he looks away, back out the window. Cars, foreign buildings, and glossy billboards swim by.

"They're kind of all bad." Too much emotion, too loudly. He presses his lips down into a thin line. There is a long silence where neither of them know what to say. Another billboard: READY TO FIND THE ONE?

"Ready to see the new apartment today?"

"Sure." Even his reflection on the window looks unconvinced.

His dad sighs. "I'm sorry. I know it's hard. If there-"

"Does mom not want me anymore?" He spits them out,

doesn't want to think about them, and the words hang out in the middle of the car, pressing up against them until there's no longer any air to breathe.

"No!" His dad stutters, awkward and clumsy as he tries to grasp them. "That's - never think that. No. Your mother and I... we just aren't right for each other anymore. It happens sometimes. But we'll always love you. You're our son."

Mocking, another billboard passes by: YOUR SOULMATE. AFFORDABLE!

His parents had used the soulmate program. They calculate the perfect person for you, a test made as accurate as possible by years of practice, and then find them for you. It makes people happy. His parents had been happy.

"You're going tomorrow, right? To the Doctor's." To find another soulmate.

"Yes." His dad glances at the rearview mirror this time, careful not to directly engage. His hope slips through anyways. His dad has been dropping hints lately. Most kids his age have already signed up.

He twists his fingers into the bottom of his shirt, worrying twists into the fabric. "Can... I go with you?"

His dad's face lights up. "Yes. Of course! You won't regret it."

"Sure."

"Really! You'll be happier. It's great timing." He grins at him through the mirror, and he gives a tentative weak one in return.

The Doctor's coat is a soft pink hue. Her presence, too, feels silken and embracing in a way that clouds his head. He misses his father a little, out in the waiting room.

"Hello. You're here today for your first check in?" Her smile at him is warm, but practiced.

"Yeah."

"Excellent!" She leans back in her chair, pulls open a drawer. "We'll begin by seeing if you're ready with our quiz. No need to worry about it. I promise it's not hard."

"Okay." He's not worried, not about the quiz. Just a formality, his father had called it. He'd gone in before him, and came out clutching a stack of papers to his chest, like they'd protect him from the rest of the world. And then you'll have these.

She pulls a paper out and then a pen. Its click echoes in the small room. "Alright! You've already filled out the general info forms, so this will be quick. Tell me, are you happy?"

He blinks, taken aback by the bluntness. "I- well, I guess, no. I'm not."

She scribbles something gently, unsurprised. "Do you feel wanted?"

There is a clock ticking in the back, and each click jumps at his thoughts, insistent to be heard. He thinks about something his mother said, way long ago, when he'd asked her why she loved his father. He makes me feel loved. Like I'm the only person in the world. She'd smiled, ruffled his hair. You'll find that too someday. Hopefully soon.

The Doctor waits for him, patient, like she knows he'll figure it out eventually.

"You can find the wrong person," he blurts. He's researched it, found countless statistics, but he can't help but ask it again.

The Doctor looks up, and gives him another practiced smile. He doesn't like it. It says nothing. "We don't. People just grow out of each other sometimes. And that's no problem! We'll just find the person you've grown into. We have a warranty for that. Barely any time spent in between feeling lost."

He thinks of the last time his parents were together. The screaming, the crying, and the loneliness of it all. "And then what?"

Her smile slips a little, confused. "Hm?"

"We grow out of each other again?"

The smile returns again. Territory she understands. "It's possible. But then we'll find someone again. Nothing to worry about."

He shakes his head. "But was I ever really wanted, then?"

She stares at him, fully lost now, and he suddenly feels very awkward. The clock keeps ticking.

She pushed her glasses up her nose. "It's - of course you were. There's just bumps in the road sometimes. But we'll find someone else again."

He can see his reflection in her glasses. He looks nervous and lost, but seeing himself grounds him. He remembers the story of Narcissus, a man cursed to love himself until he faded away. He remembers the whispers of his classmates, their horror when he'd turned down lovers, and their giggles when he'd suffered for it, enchanted into loving his reflection.

He remembers wondering what Narcissus had done, and whether it was really all that bad. In a way, he'd never been unwanted.

He stands up, a little sweaty, suddenly ready to go. "I - I think I'm going to pass for now." He feels strangely ready for an argument, and squares his shoulders, standing up as tall as he can.

The Doctor stares up at him for a second, but recovers quickly. "Oh. Okay. That's okay. You know the way back to the exit?"

He nods.

She pulls something else out of the drawer. A pamphlet. "Here. Don't be afraid to come back when you're ready. We're always happy to help."

He looks at it on the way out. More bold lettering: READY TO FIND YOUR OTHER HALF?

He tosses it into the trash. His reflection smiles at him as his father drives him home.

Will To Live

By Violet Mostek (Finalist)

My mind is fuzzy, my world dark. I'm jerked violently in and out of consciousness.

When I'm awake, I hear others shouting incoherently, my muddled mind unable to decipher the words.

Pain sears through me during the brief periods of time that it doesn't darken my mind completely. My head throbs, my entire body screaming while I try desperately to cling to consciousness. To life.

I cannot move; my limbs gripped tightly by the claws of unbearable pain. My mind is drained, body immobile.

I'm tired. So, so tired.

——

My ears feel as if they're stuffed with cotton.

I try to open my eyes or mouth, lift my head. I cannot speak or see; only hear. I can barely feel.

My thoughts rush around my head violently as I fly into a silent panic. What is happening?!

I notice all at once the constant beeping, clicking and whirring of the machines surrounding me, and I quickly pinpoint the one that is speeding up at a terrifyingly fast pace.

Is that... my heart?

My surroundings swell painfully, threatening to overcome me; to collapse over me like the wave of confusion that is already rushing through me at a dizzying pace. It's overwhelming, and all too easy to succumb to unconsciousness.

I am blanketed with calm, soft, nothingness.

——

As my consciousness slowly returns, I remember my condition with steadily increasing panic.

Questions swirl around my head at dizzying speeds. I try to decipher where I am, when suddenly it hits me.

My memories flood back, as if a dam has suddenly collapsed. They threaten to drown me, coming so fast I can barely catch a glimpse of one before it rushes past me.

I try unsuccessfully to cling to each one, but then I succeed. I latch tightly onto it; desperate to remember.

--

The sky is cloudy, dark, moon hanging low in the sky; a fruit ready to drop. It's barely visible through the clouds, which are slightly brighter where the sun will soon be.

Rain patters onto the roof of the car, and cascades down the windows in rivulets; colliding, combining, running down in a constant pattern, washing away the dirt that clings to the glass from the unpaved roads.

"Dear?" I jolt and turn to my mom as she taps my shoulder. She's smiling with her eyebrows drawn together, deepening the lines on her face.

"Yeah?"

"Did you study?"

I rub the back of my neck nervously, and she cocks an eyebrow, eyeing me sternly. Rain pours onto the windshield, heavier now. Tap tap. The windshield wipers speed up. Tap tap. Whoosh.

She goes to speak. Turns back to the road.

Her body tenses as she screams; I barely have time to widen my eyes. Headlights flash as my mom jerks the wheel, but it's too late. I hear the screech of rubber on asphalt; the crunch of cars colliding.

The airbag flies into my face, and I try to push it away, but I'm disoriented. Rain pours onto my face, soaks my shirt. I'm weakly pushing the airbag, because I can't breathe, and it hurts. Where is my mom?! Then I realize that I'm crying; terrified and confused.

Everything hurts. I want it to stop.

Suddenly, my body is jerked by another crash.

Headlights shine in the rain.

——

The machines never rest.

There is no pain, but my dreams are filled with the crunching of metal and bones. I am plagued by my mother's screams; by mine.

I often wonder about my mom. I want to know if she is okay, but no one speaks of her, and I cannot ask them.

I try to speak every time someone visits me. I try to move. I try to cry.

I wish I could cry.

——

"Alex? Can you hear me?"

A voice.

I... recognize it.

"It's Kate."

Kate?

"The doctors told us you can still hear and feel things..." the voice—Kate?—trails off and laughs nervously. Humorlessly.

She's trying to disguise a sob.

"I miss you. I wish I knew what you were thinking right now... It's going to be okay. I-I love you. God, I wish I could hear you say it back." She chokes, and something clutches my hand tightly.

"W-when the hospital called my parents, they... said you might not make it. They said you had a piece of metal—" at this, she cuts off and releases a sob heavy with grief. My heart twinges.

"Alex, I'm so glad they saved you. I love you so much. I miss—" she sobs again, and this time doesn't stop. She lays her forehead on my wrist, and her tears drip onto my hand; pool in my palm. Her head shakes with hiccups, and her breathing sounds halting and painful.

I want to comfort her. I want to stroke her hair and wrap my arms around her. I want to go to her house like I have so many times before to eat melted chocolate ice cream and watch bad movies.

I wish I could tell her that I miss her too, and I want our stupid inside jokes and constant hugs and late night sleepovers. I want to scream that she doesn't need to miss me.

I wish I wasn't stuck in this useless body.

Before I succumb to my exhaustion, I hear Kate's broken voice, whisper, "Don't give up."

— —

In Kate's wake, the hospital room is quiet. The soft beeping of Alex's heart monitor is grounding; the melody in a symphony of noises.

Alex's face is bruised and battered, and a line of stitches drags across her forehead and down the side of her nose, stopping just before it reaches her lips, hidden underneath her oxygen mask. Her broken legs, in casts, sit immobile under the thin, blue, hospital blanket. Her bandaged arms sit still on top of the blanket; cords and tubes run unencumbered to their machines.

She is outwardly battered, but her will to live is now anything but.

Viribus- A Story About Strength

By Gabriella Harris (Finalist)

The cold and unsympathetic moonlight gracefully shines on his bare skin. The man who once loved the sun envied the moon. Samual Viribus. The man who once believed in life longed for death. As he lay in bed, he reminisced about the past.

Thirteen missed calls and not one appointment made. The stubborn, yet brilliant man denies his depression. As he falls deeper into loneliness, he finds comfort in a solitary life.

"Hello, this is Dr. Pruden calling again," the answering machine reports quietly. "Please give me a call when you are ready to talk. It's been two months Mr. Viribus, let us help you."

The room grew quiet again, despite the loud cries of the traffic outside. Quiet sobs fill the cold, dark room. As the tears run down his face, the walls stare at the defeated man. A loud knock interrupts his episode and reality starts to set in. He doesn't move nor speak, no one dares to come to his home anymore. The neighborhood knows what happened to him and they stay away for a reason. However, on this cold rainy morning in Seattle, a man stands at the door with a bag full of food. His hands begin to shake. Perhaps it's the coldness, or the fear trembling in his body. The man leaves in a hurry, leaving the groceries at his brothers' door, not once looking back.

Samual lays in bed and contemplates leaving his room. When he finally does, the chilled wooden floor cools his feet. His legs begin to slightly wobble as he exits the bedroom. He hasn't left his bedroom in two weeks, let alone his bed. As he reaches for the doorknob, another knock startles him. He touches the cool metal doorknob and slowly opens the door, only to be faced with a woman. Darkness surrounds her as the sun hasn't woken up yet. The only visible features are her startling grey eyes.

"Sorry for disturbing you this early in the morning," the woman says, fishing in her bag. She brings out a manilla folder. "May I come in?"

"I'm sorry," Samual says, his mouth dry. He licks his lips. "I'm not in the right state for visitors."

He begins to close the door, but the woman places her hand on the door.

"It's about Ophelia," she says staring into his eyes. No emotion is found in her intense cool lead eyes. She hands him the folder and walks inside.

Samual doesn't move, think, or even breathe. His hands begin to shake and the folder falls to the ground. As he feels his heart beat faster he grabs onto the table to hold himself up.

Ophelia.

"My name is Detective Rogers," the woman says behind him. "If we could sit down, I would like to talk about her dea-"

"You need to leave," Samual says.

"Mr. Viribus I know this is hard but," she clears her throat and walks towards him. "This was no accident."

He turns around, red-rimmed eyes and pale-faced. His breaths become shallow and he feels as though he's going to pass out at any moment. He finds a seat in the kitchen and gulps down some water.

"The police," he begins. "They already told me everything." He looks back at the woman, tears forming. He quickly looks away.

The detective picks up the folder and takes out the contents. She places five photos in front of Samual. The room is silent as he stares at the photos. Tears run down his face as he looks at his fiances' car. A red Sudan. Polished perfectly, despite the obvious scratches and broken parts of the car.

"Why are you showing me this?" He says, not looking away from the wrecked car.

"Well, you see," she begins. "We found the other car that was involved in this hit and run."

She points to another black car on the far right side of one of the photos. Samual stops breathing. He picks up the photo with shaky hands.

"Do you know whose car this is Mr. Viribus?" The detective asks. "Do you know who killed your fiance, Ophelia?"

Various Authors

"They said," he begins, choking on his own words. "They said-"

"I know what they said," she says quietly. "But this car is registered under the name of-"

"Adam Viribus," he says barely above a whisper. "My brother."

She clears her throat again taking a deep breath. "But that isn't the only thing,"

The detective pulls out a plastic bag and takes out a note. The wrinkled piece of paper had droplets of dried bits of blood on it. "This was found in your fiances' car."

I'm so sorry Sam. I hope you can forgive me. I love you so much and I hate myself for doing this to you. I slept with him. Adam. I didn't know what I was thinking. Please forgive me, Sam. I don't know how I will face you. I love you so much and I couldn't keep it a secret anymore.

Your love, Ophelia.

The once dry paper, now coated with tears. Anger, regret, and sadness filled Samuel's hollow heart.

"Detective," Samual says slowly, fighting each syllable. "Where is he?"

The room grew quiet again, despite the early morning traffic outside. When he looked at the detective, no longer were

98

her eyes emotionless. Pity. Sadness. Sympathy. The once cold and icy grey eyes became soft.

"It seems as though," she began. "That your brother came here today." Before Samual could speak, the detective walked towards the door, opened it, and revealed a brown paper bag. A note attached.

"As I was about to knock on the door," she says. "I read the note attached." She pulls off the note and hands it to Samual.

"It's his suicide note," she says quietly.

A cold chill ran down Samuals' spine and darkness pooled his vision. Samual Viribus. The man who once believed in life longed for death. Only for death to accompany everyone but his own.

SECTION 3 – ADVENTURE

The Huntress

By Ingrid Celis (Finalist)

I took a deep breath and, using the momentum I'd gathered from running over the crenellations that lined the top of the castle's walls, flung myself towards the spiraling rooftop of the watchtower. Luckily, the torches scattered about the walls were positioned so that I was in shadow. My fingers grasped at the stony-edged parapet as I heaved myself up. Quickly, I patted myself down to make sure I hadn't lost anything in my ordeal. Bow, quiver full of arrows wrapped in waxed parchment, a map of the castle hidden in the strap of my worn leather boots, and two vials. I sighed with relief, and then started getting everything in order.

Lord Faux had told me that the advisory council and King Euclid would enter the castle's meeting hall at eight pm sharp. I glanced at the sky. I would have little time to prepare myself, but that wasn't what mattered. The only thing that did would be fulfilling the duty I'd traveled over a hundred thousand footsteps for.

I slid out my bow and set it on the cold slate floor, then removed the quiver from my shoulder. Quiet as a mouse, I unrolled the paper package inside. Inside were three thin silver-tipped arrows. I reached for the two brass vials I had in my pocket and uncorked them. I then turned the vials upside down and poured out the poison onto my arrows. To test that they were the real thing, I took a scattered leaf from the rooftop and gently wiped off leftover residue from the parchment. I gently pressed a fingertip to it. Yep, it stung.

I quickly rubbed off the drip of poison from my finger and reached for an arrow. I pulled the arrow back onto my bow carefully, acting as if it was made of spider thread. With it loaded, I tested it out on my string, drawing it back a few times, trying to fully come to terms with what I was about to do. Would I really be—

Suddenly, I heard footsteps echoing against the stone corridors below. Gently, I set down my bow and crept over to the parapet. Under me, there was a squadron of guards making their nightly rounds. I tiptoed back to the center of the rooftop. They would be the last people out tonight other than the council and the king, according to Faux. I held my knees and listened for the sound of their feet marching away.

After I was sure that they had left, I stood up and paced the granite space, staying away from the parapet so I wouldn't be seen. The sky had turned into an inky landscape, and scattered stars twinkled down at my rooftop. I felt so small and insignificant, compared to the masterpiece above me. Then I made a fist.

You know who deserves to feel insignificant? whispered a small voice in my head. Him. He's led this kingdom to ruin, and thrown all of the city-states into debt. This is your chance to save the whole country; that's why you agreed to—

I shook my head to clear my thoughts. No emotions, I chastised myself. Or else you won't perform.

Muffled voices and footsteps snapped me out of my reverie. I grabbed my bow, no longer caring about my noise level, as I peered down toward the castle's inner curtain wall by the entryway. With the numerous torches lining the inside of the castle, I could make out the figures of the advisory council, fanned in front of and behind who I presumed to be the king. I gripped my bow and moved my index finger and thumb to the fletching of my arrow.

The miniscule group of royals stopped in the middle of the path. They seemed to be arguing about something. The king tried to continue into the palace, but a noble touched his arm, and they continued to stand in the same location. There was no second to lose.

I crouched by the parapet of the tower and drew back my bowstring to my full arm span. I steadied my recurve and stared down at the king through my right eye. I took a deep, quiet breath, then released the tension on my bow with an imperceptible, gentle twang.

My positioning was perfect. The arrow's path drooped just enough to hit its target. The king, like a doll figure, flopped over onto the cold ground, far below. Seconds after the arrow left death in its wake, screams from the council echoed against the tall walls. A figure that I assumed was Faux started gesturing towards the dead king and the doors into the meeting hall.

I watched from my perch as Lord Faux and the advisory council surrounded King Euclid's body and carried it further into the castle. I knew Faux would want me to go back to his house to discuss payment. With the deed done, I turned, and, grabbing the evidence, I raced off the parapet into the night.

Order

By Sam Mutschler-Aldine (Finalist)

The sun peered through a slit in the drapes. It cast a line of warm light, scanning the room as time passed, until it rested on Ray's eyes. He woke, startled by the bright red color of his eyelids. This was the only effective method the world had of stirring him from his comforters. Every day Ray set out to open the slit spitefully, stumbling over his various possessions strewn across the floor. Every day the two cloth pieces whipped apart, and every day the boy would stare out at the light until his eyes adjusted. This particular day was stunning. In fact, the weather outside his room never ceased to be perfect. Unfortunately, every day when the blinding occurred, and the clumsiness ensued, and the eyes adjusted, they met bars. Rusted steel rods in such tight columns only a sliver of the outside world shone through. Ray had given up spying through the crack by this point in his life, the glare only contributed to his splitting headache. The small glimpse into what possibilities might lay just beyond the bars had turned promise to torture. An overwhelming sense of missed opportunity cracked down upon his skull as a gavel does a sounding block. He made a silent display of frustration, whipping the drapes back to their original state. He traced his steps back in the dark as he did every day. He tripped over an unidentifiable object as usual, and let his body flop into the dark blue crater resembling his figure on the cot. He clung to his comforters and drifted off. The line was on the wall now, over Ray's head. It would scan the other faces of the room in his slumber. It would come back around. It would rest on his eyes. It was routine.

Malice

By Ryleigh Moule (Finalist)

The tune of a child's laughter sways through the branches of the forest, echoing off the nearby cave. Athel would gladly face immense danger in order to protect her son. Closing her eyes, Athel pictures her little boy; his blond hair, and curious eyes steady her shaking hands and calm her heart.

It wasn't long before her child was born that Athel experienced her first vision of him. She saw a happy, normal childhood. However, these visions grew increasingly worrisome. As her son would grow, he would be thrown into battle, losing his life. And so, with a heavy heart, Athel knew that she could not let this fate come to fruition. She knew that she must face the malice before it could develop into an unstoppable force. And as the fates balanced, she knew it was now time.

Adorning Athel's hair are a few braids, placed to keep flying strands out of her vision. The traditional champion's tunic is pulled on, boots are fastened, and a cloak is donned. She will be traveling light up through the mountain. Strapped onto her back, Athel carries a finely crafted warriors bow, an abundance of arrows, and a magnificent sword of legends that once glowed with the blessings of the goddess.

Athel faces the mountain. From here she will be leaving her small camp and traveling into the cursed hideaway.

Entering the cave, Athel moves silently. If there happened to be any followers of the wicked nearby, it would be a mistake to make them aware of her presence. A steady thrumming fills her ears. Athels heart races.

The first part of the trip progressed rather quickly. Though she had yet to run into an enemy search party, the eerie sounds of the cave filled with the slow, steady drips of water kept her on edge. The chill of the cool air seeps into her bones. Icicles embellish the stone walls. Breaths are visible in the surrounding air.

Athel enters a clearing, rubbing her sore, frozen hands. Hearing a grunt, Athel whips her head up to see the camp she had just stumbled into. A small group of skeletons, who had been previously gathered around a fire, scramble to grab their weapons after spotting the warrior. Gripping her sword, Athel charges the enemies. Slicing, dodging, and parrying, Athel fights vehemently. After defeating them, Athel makes sure to release the tainted spirits within.

Collapsing in exhaustion, she crawls toward the small, crackling fire. The flames chase away the deep seated chill. Feeling relatively safe by the crepitating fire, Athel drifts into a slumber.

Stretching, Athel's muscles ache. The fortress of rocks and stone comes into view as she peels open her eyes. Only a few dimly glowing coals of the fire remain. Athel pulls herself to her feet.

Nearby lay Athel's discarded sword. She examines the blade before sheathing it. Glancing around, Athel notices a small crack in the wall above her. This would be the only way to get into the main chamber.

Approaching the wall, she begins the climb. A squeak escapes her lips, echoing in the distance as she loses a bit of her footing, the rock crumbling below her and smashing onto the ground. Athel's icy fingers were beginning to have a hard time holding on. Quickly scurrying up the remaining length of the wall, Athel reaches a ledge where she is able to catch her breath. The crack leading to the main chambers stands only a few feet away.

Steeling her nerves, Athel prepares to squeeze through the entrance. Her fear of small spaces would not be her breaking point. She climbs through. Arms and legs scrape rocks, leaving small cuts. She begins to hyperventilate. Eyes water. The room closes in. Walls of rock push back. Teeth grind. Her head pulses. Her body wiggles, looking for an escape. And, finally, her head emerges on the other side. Athel pauses, breathing heavily and attempts to calm herself down. She pulls the rest of her body through the opening.

Athel takes in the open space and tall ceiling before her. The overall cavern is rounded with large ice spikes concentrated toward the perimeter of the room. An opening in the ceiling is in view, moonlight streaming through. A large figure huddles on the opposing side of the room.

Scales glisten in the pale moonlight. It was clear that this is where the malice was originating from. Releasing this beast from the demon would ensure her son's survival. Athel draws her bow, aiming straight for the dragon's head. Her only thoughts being about saving her son from his fate. Flickering and gleaming, the creature's eyes open, staring back at her.

She releases the arrow.

A blood curdling shriek.

Silence.

The dragon is still. Pouring from the poor creature's mouth came the malice, deep red with piercing, glowing eyes. She draws her sword and lunges for the fog like being. The warrior attacks the demon's physical form. She parries at every possible opportunity, unfortunately still taking some devastating hits. The being weakened with every hit, and so did the warrior.

A child's cry breaks through the sounds of battle, slicing through the air. Tears fill the mother's eyes. Athel knew it was time. She holds the sword outstretched before her, pointing at the malice several paces away. And the goddess has mercy. Intense glowing, emanating from the sword, floods the room with light. One more devastating hit and the being is no more.

Athel falls to the ground, kneeling as the light of the sword dies out.

The dragon opens its eyes once more. The malice has been banished from this land. Having grown old and tired, the dragon had allowed the evil to take over. The air stills. The mountain's cold cavern, which once reeked of evil, now felt a sense of peace. Athel drops the sword, metal clanking against the stone floor.

The mother smiles and begins to cry. She will be able to see her son again.

A Passionate Lamentation

By Emma Khoury (Finalist)

Her fingers grasped the thick papyrus, delicately turning the rough surface that danced with ink scribbles. She opened her eyes in amazement; finally, she had been able to get her hands on a codex. She would read about philosophy, geometry, maybe even-

"Scintilla! Excita!" She could hear her mother yelling from the kitchen. Rubbing her eyes, she found herself back in reality, in pitch darkness. Her small house in the idyllic countryside did not come with windows like many of the magistrate's mansions in Rome, so Scintilla started and ended her day in darkness. After putting on her tunic, she felt around in the obscurity for her wooden belt, that would keep her toga snug around her slender hips as she went out to do morning chores. Scintilla ventured out in the rising horizon wearing her old leather sandals.

After milking the cows, feeding the sheep, and picking

some fresh wheat and olives for tomorrow's breakfast, Scintilla embraced her mother, who was making breakfast for Scintilla's father.

"Salvete, mater," she greeted. "Quid est jentaculo?"

"Cur facet rogas ubi noscis jam quid habebis?" Mater said, smiling, as she kneaded bread for tomorrow. Scintilla realized her mother raised a good point: she already knew what her life schedule. She always had the same breakfast, bread with honey and dates; she went outside to do the same old chores, and she usually had the same dinner with her parents. Scintilla dreamt of adventure, of chasing her dreams to become a scholar and study philosophy, geometry, and astronomy. 'Yeah, sure, Scintilla, that'll happen," she thought to herself, chewing angrily, feeling the coarse wheat scrape against her tongue. Her mother, of course, was oblivious to Scintilla's thoughts. With a sigh, Scintilla finished her breakfast and went out to join her father in the fields, giving him a chance to eat breakfast.

The sun was now rising with its full strength, and Scintilla basked in this glorious light as she picked grapes from the vineyard. With all menial tasks, the mind starts to wander, and Scintilla's mind often concerned with her unfulfilled dreams. It was not fair. How come Quintus, her older brother, got to travel to Rome and study under the greatest minds, like Pliny the Elder, when she was just as smart as her older role model? It was not fair, especially not for women in the Roman empire, Scintilla thought. Disgust coursed through her veins, giving her the desire to counteract the most powerful men in the empire, but what she made up in ideals, she lacked in strength.

With her wooden basket filled with dark bunches of grapes, each individual grape lost amid the masses, Scintilla lamented how her life was so similar to these grapes as she dropped them in the winepress. Every roman farmer cultivates and provides food for their families, however, all individuality is lost amid the masses of people and territories in the empire, under Caesar. 'If only I could do something about this!' Scintilla reflected passionately. She stacked the purple-stained wood along with the others under the giant olive tree that no longer bore olives. A shame, yet it made for a great place to house farm equipment and tools that did not fit among the rest that was by the back of the brick foundation. Scintilla checked with her mother if she needed anything ("nil, gratia," she smiled warmly) and decided to take Argus for a walk in the nearby woods.

Argus was a beautiful dog, but more importantly, he was Scintilla's best friend, loyal to her even when everyone forgot about her. His copper fur glinted in the sunlight, and his black eyes served as a mirror that always seemed to reflect the happiest version of herself, even when that was farthest from the truth. Today, as she looked beneath Argus' eyelashes in that one-way mirror, she saw a happy spark in her eyes.

Spark.

Scintilla.

They were equivalent, meaning the same thing. But what is a spark if there is nothing nearby to ignite? What is a dream without anyone or anything to propel you towards it? Scintilla could feel herself tumbling in an internal black hole as she walked through the forest. Reality shifted back and forth from an internal monologue to her surroundings. Trees seemed to reach up to the sky, mocking her, shouting and laughing "WE CANNOT HEAR YOU FROM DOWN BELOW, SO FAR, FAR

AWAY!". Why can't I go to Rome, and study? Tree branches struck her arm, stealing away the passion from before. I am just as smart as Quintus, but what do I do? Stay home to prepare for marriage. Leaves fell into her hair, and all she could hear above the wind was Argus's concerned whines. I will never have a chance to prove myself. At this realization, she dropped to her knees, ignoring the scratches on her arm and the trees' mockery. She was tumbling faster down a black hole, losing sight of reality. It was all becoming an illusion. She tasted saltwater on her lips, and she could feel Argus' rough tongue against the wet surface of her skin. Losing sight, plunging farther and deeper into a dark expanse, Scintilla uttered one last cry: "Quid?"

Why?

Stitches

By McKenna Mitcham (Finalist)

One evening, when I was 4 years old, I was playing in the middle of the living room, ringed in by an old wooden bench, the television, and my dad sitting on the leather couch. As I sat on the worn carpet playing with my dolls, I could faintly hear the sound of rain outside, pattering against the window, and multiple explosion scenes from my dad's movie. My three-year-old brother was smashing his toy cars against each other and running them along the edge of the bench. With his short attention span, he quickly got bored with his cars and moved on to his dinosaurs.

Not long after, Holden decided, yet again, that he wanted to do something else. Approaching me, he announced, "I can do circles faster than you."

Being so highly competitive, I responded, "No you can't! I can go WAY faster than you because I'm older!"

To show him that I could clearly whirl around in circles faster than him, I jumped to my feet, clutching my plush, life-size Strawberry Shortcake doll. Just as I began to twirl, my father warned, "Stop spinning before you get hurt," under a mouthful of salty popcorn. Ignoring this, I continued to spin, hand-in-hand with my doll. Again, I heard my father grunt in annoyance at my antics and tv blocking, "I told you to stop. The living room isn't big enough for you to do that."

Though he said this just a moment too late, as my foot slipped out from underneath me, and gravity flung me into the edge of the nearby wooden bench. Covering the left side of my face with my hand, tears brimming in my eyes with shock, I asked my dad if I was bleeding. The pain had not occurred to me yet, as I only felt a slight tingling sensation.

"I told you-you were going to get hurt," he sighed, "but no, you're fine. It's only a little red around your cheek. You'll probably have a pretty big bruise tomorrow."

Sighing with relief, I lowered my hand. Feeling a thick layer of sliminess, I looked down. Struck with terror, I realized that my hand was soaked in blood. A moment later, more blood came rushing out, squirting in intervals next to my eye. My dad, frozen in his seat, petrified at the blood, took a moment before jumping up. He grabbed a handful of paper towels and smothered my face with them. While holding the coarse paper against my head, he frantically told my brother to get me ice. Though, my brother was much too small to reach the ice on his own and struggled. My father quickly got the ice on his own and directed me to stay put and hold the items to my face. As he ran to get his wallet and keys and call my mother, I snuck into the bathroom to see how bad the injury really was. With one glance in the mirror, I saw the deep gash, with ripped skin flayed up around it. It was then, that I felt the pain. I let out a blood-curdling scream, as my face suddenly felt like cheese being violently grated, and the smell of pennies filled my nostrils. My dad sprinted into the bathroom, grabbed my arm, pulled me hastily into the car, and rushed to the ER.

Just minutes after walking through the hospital doors, swarms of nurses hurried to my side, taking me into a different room, and began to clean the area around the wound with a strong chemical. In so much pain, I continued to scream as they wiped away at the trauma.

"No way I'm letting you put a needle in my face!" I yelped at the nurse.

"We're gonna need the burrito," I heard her whisper to another nurse.

A few minutes later, the doctor took me into another room, with frightening tools laid out on a silver platter and a table at the center. Laid across the table was a thick, tough cloth with long cordage at the end. Scared, I took a step back towards the door, but a nurse grabbed me around the waist and forced me onto the table, where I was laid down on top of the fabric. Swiftly, they wrapped the cloth around me and secured it with the cordage. I guess this was the burrito that they were talking about. Without any anesthesia, the doctors went to work on my face. Slowly, the doctor sent his thick needle deep into my flesh. The tug of the string through a piece of my skin sent a howl from deep within my gut. Ten times. Ten times, the doctor drove his pointed stick into my wound, burrowing down further than the previous, the nylon sliding around under my skin and coming out the other side of my laceration. Each time it was threaded across, I could feel the skin around it becoming tighter and tighter. And with each stitch, I let out a banshee shriek.

Finally, the doctor finished, untied me, and helped me down from the table. Quickly glancing around, I made a dash for the door, afraid that I was going to be forced down and tortured again. Just outside the room was my dad, who greeted me with a big bear hug.

Before I left, one of the nurses approached me and said, "You did great in there! Do you want a treat for your boo-boo?"

With my head hanging low, dried blood and tears streaked across my face, I slightly nodded in acceptance. Moments later, I was given a cherry popsicle to soothe my sore throat from all of my wailing and sent home.

The Legend of the Tifflewick Brew

By Jace Ballard (Finalist)

Long long long long long long long ago, deep in the thick forbidden forests, in a giant fortress, lived a small hairy bush dwarf named Sultan. He lived alone, all alone. His family had all died in the past due to Ticky Wicky Fever, so now he was the only one left of his kind.

Ticky Wicky Fever was always very dangerous to anyone who dared touch the Ticky Wicky Hicky Plant, which grows near rivers and swamps. Sultan's family went out one morning and grew very hungry and delirious, they went down to the river for a drink (not noticing the Ticky Wicky Hicky Plant next to them), they caught the fever. The fever makes you feel just fine but the insides of the body collapse within, the last smell you're able to smell is of course the sweet sweet smell of the Ticky Wicky.

Sultan found a wizard, who had been traveling, he hired him to dispose of his family magically and with honor. The wizard agreed. Within the hour, Sultan's family were buried and well taken care of. Sultan paid the wise man twenty fings, and sent him on his way. The wizard wasn't seen around the parts for quite a while, until one day he made his rounds again and stopped by the lonely bush dwarf's home.

Sultan and the wizard became quick friends and they shared a nice cup of Ant Punch every time he came around to his place. But this time, Sultan asked to go with the wizard. The wizard agreed and the two of them made their way to the kingdom. The markets were very busy, the day of the king's birthday was at hand. Many of the children gathered around the great wizard and asked him to do his magic. He grinned and nodded. He sprouted gold silvery light from his magical staff, which would make wheezing and popping sounds the whole way.

The children laughed and applauded, the wizard turned to Sultan and introduced him to the crowd of youngins. Some of the kids thought his beard was funny and how he was just as tall as most of them there. Sultan, trying to make the kids laugh like they did with the wizard, made funny faces and actions. They all enjoyed his performance, the wizard even grinned.

They waved goodbye to their admirers and steered their way up to the king's palace. The king was very happy to see the great wizard and wished to see his tricks. But before the wizard went to his work, he introduced the bush dwarf to his majesty.

The king was shocked, he had never seen anything like Sultan before. He circled him and grazed in amazement. He asked the dwarf what land he was from and if there was more of himself. Sultan explained what had happened to his family.

"Ticky Wicky Hicky Plant you say? I'm afraid I am not acquainted with the species. Tell me, are they good in stews?"

the king asked.

"No no, sir. You never never want a ticky in your belly, no no sir." Sultan replied.

"I see no threat to me, after all I am the king of this fair land and I will have this ticky wicky you speak of."

"No, no fair king. His majesty will not have such a plant. Impossible! Impossible humble king."

The king caressed his chin and then asked the dwarf to make a stew for his birthday consisting of a Ticky Wicky Hickey Plant or he shall be executed. With no choice at all, the dwarf bowed and left with the wizard. Together, they set off on their way back to the thick forest of Sultan's home.

Sultan got right to work on making the special stew fit for his majesty. He lifted off fings, hings, and jings off his shelves full of marshy onions and swelsh seasonings. Fish cheddars and barge maker powders, he plummeted them into a smoking pot. The wizard looked very unsure at what his little friend was doing.

"You're not killing the king are you?" he asked, concerned.

"Of course not, I don't kill."

"But he ordered you to put the plant in the stew."

"Yes, but I will be loyal to his majesty and hope he won't die sir. Therefore I shalt not kill the sire. But I will make a stew." the dwarf assured.

The wizard offered to help, Sultan agreed, and together they made the stew into a brew. They threw in peas and corn, sticks and bits, things and wings. Stirring mouse spits, tentacle pits, and rhino jits; just for some flavor. The wizard sprinkled in cat furs, lures, and purrs while Sultan chopped the shreds of gillywheat and spicy chicken feet. Within moments the stew was ready for a magical start.

The wizard said his wise words, "Hemmy Hemmy Marshy Shred, turn this Stew into Brew!" A dash of red silk sprang from the edge of his staff and into the pot. Sultan mixed the brew until it became a gold grimson blue. "Alas, I call it Tifflewick Brew!"

The wizard grinned, within minutes they were packed up and were there at the king's tables. The king applauded their big achievement. Sultan assured the king that there WAS the Ticky Wicky Plant in the brew. With that, the king dished himself a bowl and gulped it right down. To the wizard and the dwarf's surprise, the king fell off his chair clutching his stomach, within seconds the king was dead. The butler charged forward, "What was in that!?"

"Just corn and peas and-."

"The king was allergic to corn! You, you killed his majesty!" the butler bent down on one knee, "Thank you! Thank you! Behold, the legend has spoken that one will come forth and kill his majesty by complete and total accident. He who does so, will be appointed the next king of the land! Hail his majesty! Hail the Tifflewick! Long live the new king!"

The Mat

By Corinne de Syon (Finalist)

Everything was burning. The smell was horrible. I groaned and struggled for breath; I could feel the end nearing, and I thought please, just let it end...

I collapsed onto the mat, arms burning from my final push up. Despite the exhaustion consuming my muscles, I rolled over to avoid the pungent smell of stale sweat emanating from the old mat. With enormous effort, I began to control my breathing, just as Coach walked over to me.

"Get on up," she said. "Time to start practice."

I couldn't believe I had gotten myself into this mess again – for the third time this week. Being late to swim practice used to be comical, if not slightly embarrassing; now, it was simply torture. One minute late and it was five push ups; five minutes late and it was twenty. On that unfortunate day, it had been twenty; I had never been so glad to jump into a freezing, over chlorinated pool just seconds later.

Today, however, was a different story. I had organized everything so as to be ten minutes early to swim practice – I wouldn't touch that warm-up mat until at least next week. I had checked my watch obsessively since I had gotten home from school; today was Monday, and I was motivated.

I knew I had to leave by 6:15 pm to get there with an overly ample amount of time. But suddenly, after looking up from a particularly thorny math problem, I realized it was 6:20.

I rushed to the bathroom to take out my contact lenses. Then, the inevitable: I misplaced my glasses after throwing away my daily contacts. As I stumbled around searching frantically for some form of sight, I stubbed my toe harder than I would have thought possible. I screeched louder than anyone within a five-mile radius thought possible.

Then hopping on one foot, I located my glasses and checked my watch. 6:24 pm! I was horrified. And I wasn't even changed yet – I was supposed to be at swim practice at this very moment, chatting with my friends and breathing a sigh of relief that I was avoiding The Mat. I tore down the stairs to the laundry room, searching through the pile of swim equipment for my blue swimsuit.

6:25.

As I rocketed back up the steps, I shouted up to my dad – I had been dreading this point. My dear father likes to take his time getting ready for the aerobics class he attends while I swim, located in the same complex as the pool. This entails packing everything from the earbuds to the exercise ball, without forgetting the pads for his knees or the car keys. At this point, walking would be quicker.

6:26. I changed into my suit so fast you would have thought there was a tornado coming.

I rushed downstairs, grabbed everything I needed, and begged my dad to hurry up. He was so slow at tying his shoelaces. I raced to the car and almost tripped as I threw myself into the passenger seat. At this point, my dad understood without needing to ask – I had often recounted the horrors of the punishment push ups and The Mat in excruciating detail. He pressed down on the gas pedal before we even had time to buckle in.

"Come on, speed up!" I urged him.

But then came the most dreaded thing of all. The red light at the corner right before the pool parking lot. This particular red light was infamous in our family. It had delayed my sister's arrival to her State-level vocal competition and even almost made my dad miss the interview for his first job. This red light and my family had history.

I sat back in my seat, defeated. I knew it was almost over, but I couldn't yet resign myself to the thought of The Mat.

It was 6:29.

After what seemed like forever, the light turned green. We half-parked, I busted out of the car, yelled, "thanks, Dad!" And ran as fast as I could to the entrance of the pool.

I swung open the heavy door and glanced over towards the tall glass panes through which you could see the pool – and did a double take. The pool was deserted. The lights were off. There was nobody here except for a couple of college students working at the front desk. I ran down the ramp and looked around the corner. I looked around, breathing hard. No one. I went up to the balcony as if in a trance. Again, no one. I looked at my watch – 6:31 pm. I had gotten there just barely on time – I had avoided The Mat – but I had no energy to celebrate; I was utterly confused. Why was no one here?

And then I remembered.

It was President's Day. There was to be no swim practice for the Piranha Swim Club on President's Day. A feeling of pure defeat, mixed with anger and helplessness, overcame me and pushed me against the wall. I slid slowly down to the ground, breathing harder than after any set, muscles aching more than from any punishment push ups. Both my brain and body were jelly. My stubbed toe was aching again. No swim. I picked myself up as slower than a sloth would have and walked back towards the front doors.

My dad was just coming in the gym doors; he looked at me with bewilderment. I had no words. He seemed to understand after a moment; he embraced me and said, with a hint of a smile, "At least you avoided The Mat."

Tuatha Dé Danann

By Julaisa E. Santiago (Finalist)

I take a deep breath and run, a full sprint to feel something physical. Don't trip, please don't trip, I hope, eyeing the ground, stepping my feet over branches, and lifting my other foot up as soon as the other hits the leaves. I ran straight to not lose my way; eventually my sight reached its favorite place. An opening in a perfect square shape.

My excited eyes ignored the ground and that's when my foot kicked a tree's root and my body was plummeting to the ground. Bracing myself for impact, my eyes closed, yet it never came. I was breathing heavily and refused for my eyes to open. Did I die? I thought, a shiver running through my body. My lungs hurt; death isn't supposed to hurt. Opening my left eye I let out a scream; I was staring at the dead leaves, the ground. My body was floating. I put my hand over my mouth and whimpered, I was shaking.

My body collapsed to the ground, rolling over and removing the dirt from my face I looked around quickly, pulling out my hunter's knife. I scrambled to get up and held it close. I moved towards the square-shaped area with the on-edge feeling of paranoia to look behind me.

I place the knife on my thigh as I sit, wondering what happened to me. Was it a hallucination? It's possible that I did hit my head, but my head doesn't hurt, does it? I bring my hand up to my head and trace my fingers around, hoping for crimson liquid on my fingers, but there was nothing. Does crazy run in the family? I look around again. I'm losing it, aren't I? It's happened to mam and now it's happening to me! I stand and turn, coming face to face with an adorable-looking girl with leaves in her light brown hair, elvish ears, and iridescent wing shapes on her back. I could not help but stare at her and she stared right back at me. A wooden staff popped up in her hand and I quickly picked up my knife from the ground taking a defensive stance. I really am a crazy person.

"You're not allowed here!" she exclaimed.

"Not 'allowed'?" I'm confused. "It's a forest, you eejit. I can come here whenever I want! At least I'm not pretending to be a defender of the woodlands, dressing as a whole fairy." I scoff. A small gasp comes out of her mouth and she shakes her head.

"I don't know who you are, and you do not know who I am. Go on back where you came from." I rolled my eyes. "It's not safe for you here anyway. And exactly what are you going to do with that knife, kill me? Amateur move, dear." Gee, so intimidating coming from a short girl dressed as a fairy!

"Would my leaving make you feel that much better?" I ask,

putting my arm down and relaxing my stance. I see her nod her head and smile; I smile back at her. "Right, okay. Well." I sit down in front of her. "If that's the case, I'm not leaving," I say with a grin and then look at her seriously. "It's a forest! You know what a forest is? I can be here if I want to! It's not a private area!" I exclaim, hoping to get through her thick skull.

"You leave me no other choice," She says, a scowl on her face. I roll my eyes as I watch her raise her staff and arm in the air. She hits the bottom of her staff on the ground and begins to chant in a familiar language, but I did not know it fluently.

I stand and grab my knife when I hear ruffles of leaves, the girl yells out names and that's when I heard loud snarls and cries similar to ones of a big cat. A big black panther was approaching me on the right, another to my left, and another accompanied each. Time to book it.

I turn quickly and run, holding my knife as I move my arms swiftly. I knew I wouldn't be able to survive, but shoot, a girl could try. I aimed towards a row of trees and climbed faster than I thought I could. I noticed the big cats beginning to climb as well and I jump to the other tree and jump to any available. I felt as if I was gliding through air, gravity didn't seem to have a pull on me. The cats reacted quickly, but now one was stuck in a tree. I finally got to the point where I could jump down. The snarls were deafening; I looked behind me, the cougar no more than five feet away. I spin my head back and felt my foot kick a rock embedded in the ground, I flew into the air.

I'm truly dead this time around, the cats are going to devour me, my body is going to rot here. Mam and papa will find my body messed up and disoriented, I thought, with despair in my heart; I never felt the ground collide with my body. No claws or sharp teeth sunk into my thigh, and it was quiet. I was staring at the ground again. Dead leaves, dirt, broken branches... I gulped. A few seconds later, my body finally fell, face planting on the ground. I sat up, leaning over and coughing, spitting due to the dirt in my mouth. There was a crimson liquid trickling down my arm.

I heard a small snarl and glanced up, noticing four stray cats staring at me, but they ran away. I got up, ignoring the pain and dripping. I started speed walking home. "Do not return, human." I heard a soft, chilling voice echo from the back of my head and felt a light breeze blow.

Woodrow West; The Cactus Dragon

By Aidan Evans (Finalist)

In a town known as Spitbucket, lives a sheriff and his deputy, Woodrow and Stick. These two live slightly outside of town. Woodrow and Stick aren't very smart, they spend most of their days in the saloon talking about tall tales such as The Legend of The Cactus Dragon. While in the saloon Woodrow once again describes the first time he saw The Cactus Dragon.

"So, I was out in the desert looking for bandits, and I look over only to see this giant flying snake eating a cact-,"

Stick interrupted, "There is no way you saw a flying snake, they don't even have wings!"

"What do you know Stick, you ain't never left Spitbucket."

"I have, I once went to Alabama to visit my cousin Cactus." Stick countered.

"There is no way you have a cousin in Alabama named Cactus!"

A man wearing a raccoon hat walks into the saloon and says, "Hey, it's my good old cousin Stick!" Stick looked back only to see Cactus, his cousin from Alabama.

"What are you doing here Cactus?" Stick said.

"I came to move in with my cousin," Cactus responded.

Woodrow interrupted the conversation, "Can I continue my story?"

Stick responded, "Fine, but not through dialog." Woodrow continued, he told the two of The Cactus Dragon and how it likes to eat cacti. He said that was a bad thing because instead of the wild west, they would live in The Sahara Desert because all of the cacti were gone. "Therefore we must go on a hunt for this Cactus Dragon and kill it!" said Woodrow.

They all went to bed, for in the morning they go on a hunt for The Cactus Dragon...

Woodrow explained that they first had to find The Desert Tortoise. "The Desert Tortoise is a tortoise that wanders The Wild West, waiting for travelers it can give it's knowledge to."

"So, you're just going to risk our lives in the hope that there's some kind of turtle out in the desert?" Cactus asked.

"Well yeah." Woodrow answered.

"Cool, I'm in!" Cactus exclaimed.

The three spent hours and hours walking in the desert, but they never found anything.

They went back to Spitbucket upset about their failure. Just then, a tortoise walked into the saloon. Woodrow saw it was The Desert Tortoise. The Desert Tortoise told them to follow him, so they did. The walk was slow and exhausting, but eventually, they found The Cactus Dragon's home. When Woodrow walked up to the door, it opened automatically. As they walked in, the sound of Cactus screaming slowly disappeared.

"It knows we're here..." Woodrow said faintly as he pulled out his shotgun.

They continued into the cave, after walking in the darkness for a while they saw a shimmer of light in the distance. They started walking towards it. "It's a torch Woodrow!" Stick exclaimed. Stick grabbed the torch, but instead of it coming off the wall, it acted as a lever, a bunch of torches lit up to reveal that they were in a temple, the Cactus Dragon Temple of legend.

The walls were made of stone with moss all over the walls. Carved into the walls were drawings and words of a forgotten time. "From these pictures, I would guess that people acted like this thing was a god." Woodrow said. Stick didn't respond, he just pointed while his hand was shaking. "What is it Stick?' Woodrow asked and then he looked to where he was pointing. It was a silhouette of a giant snake, but this wasn't just a snake, it was the Cactus Dragon. The beast had awoken and stood 20 feet tall and its skin was green with black spots all over.

"I think we're done for Stick." Woodrow said.

"I don't know about you, but I'm going to just, RRRRUUUUUUNNNNN!!!!!" Stick exclaimed while leaving Woodrow in the dust. The both of them started running while the Cactus Dragon started to slither towards them at immense speed.

"IT'S GAINING ON US STICK!!!" Woodrow screamed.

The beast's tail whipped around and blocked the entrance, they were trapped. Woodrow, trying to find a way out, frantically started to shoot at the Cactus Dragon.

"Wait! Did you load your gun with blanks again?!" Stick exclaimed.

"Oh shoot, I did." Woodrow said.

"We're done for, bye Woodrow." Stick said while going into the fetal position.

Then when all hope was lost, a figure came jumping out of nowhere and grabbed onto the Cactus Dragon's head yanking it back, it was Cactus.

"CACTUS!" Woodrow and Stick exclaimed.

The Cactus Dragon started to bang it's head against walls to try to get Cactus off but he wouldn't let go. Woodrow and Stick ran for the exit when the floor broke underneath them and they fell into a tunnel. Cactus fell off and landed next to them.

"We better get to running." Stick said

They started running, but the Cactus Dragon was following. They kept running when they saw light in the distance.

"Look! Light!" Woodrow exclaimed.

They started getting closer and closer, and the Cactus

Dragon was getting ready to consume them. The three of them jumped into the light then there was a BOOM! The Cactus Dragon was gone and the three of them were in Woodrow's outhouse

"Hold on?" Woodrow said, "The Cactus Dragon had a tunnel that went into my outhouse!"

"I guess that would explain the creepy noises I would hear when I was using it." Stick replied.

"I don't know about you guys, but I'm gonna head to the saloon and try to forget this ever happened." Cactus said.

After all that, they weren't able to defeat The Cactus Dragon, but they at least got an adventure out of it, and maybe this experience will help them in the future...

A Peek into the Future

By Reeja Khan (Finalist)

The time machine rattled violently. My eyes squinted through the unbearable beam of light, and I clenched my fists. Seconds later, the light became dull and the machine stopped moving. I stepped out of the humming time device and looked at the board in front of me broadcasting the current date in bold. January 1st, 2030. As I walked around, I caught a glimpse of the news on the digital screen that was placed on one of the skyscrapers. The news read "Attention: Red Wolves joining the list of extinct animals along with Florida Grasshopper sparrows, and tigers. Beginning of the sixth era of mass extinction"

As a person who has empathy for all living things and utter respect for life itself, this news was devastating. Additionally, as humans with intellect, it is our duty to protect the rights of animals who rely on us and cannot stand up for themselves. To learn more about the news, I walked into one of the digital public libraries and sat in front of one of the virtual screens and began to search for articles related to animal extinction. Hours passed, and I read 200 articles which is more than what I have read in 17 years of my life. Every article contained one common phrase: "Anthropogenic activities." One of the articles stated that in 2024 in response to global economic collapse, many countries legalized animal poaching as long as the government of that country received 30% of the profits. While the economy thrived, several endangered species of animals rapidly began to go extinct. As I read through the article, I began to question the presence of humanity in people. I could never imagine that there will be a time when the upcoming generations will have to learn about these animals in the same context as we learned about dodos. While the human-caused animal extinction deprived children of an amusing childhood, it also tempered with the natural course of life and disrupted the environment. After pondering on the situation and feeling devastated, I realized that I could prevent mass animal extinctions if I could warn the nations back in 2020 about it.

In the next 12 months, I collected several articles related to the legalization of poaching, recordings of news that stated the extinctions of different species of animals, and interviews of politicians who supported legal poaching and credible activists who explained the consequences of it.

When I went back to the year 2020, I contacted the United Nations. At first, they thought I needed to see a psychiatrist when I told them that I have been to the future. After several failed attempts at setting a meeting with the United Nations, I realized that to be taken seriously by the organization, all I had to do was draw enough attention to my case. To do so, I used several social media platforms. For example, I used TikTok, which is a very popular social platform to make videos explaining all the evidence that helped my case gain popularity.

After being broadcasted in the news several times, I was contacted by the United Nations and was asked to present my evidence to them. Eventually, I showed them the heartbreaking evidence from the future. For example, I presented articles from 2030 stating the long list of extinct animals caused by the legalization of poaching in 2024 and other anthropogenic activities. Moreover, I also presented anecdotes of children from the future explaining how they wished to see the extinct animals in person. With the use of credible evidence and igniting emotions of empathy, I succeeded in explaining the environmental consequences and ethical issues regarding animal cruelty. Moreover, I appealed to several global leaders to create stricter policies that will ensure the prevention of human greed from harming animals or there will come a time when there will be forests, but no animals to live in them.

In the Future

By Chad Jordan (Finalist)

On a late Sunday night, I reclined on my couch. It was a quiet night like any other; I could hear the crickets chirping their tunes outside my house. I let the low, chattering voices on the TV soothe me to sleep that night. I closed my eyes and, minutes later, reopened them to a place that I did not recognize but filled me with a sense of nostalgia.

I heard a familiar voice call out to me, ""breakfast is ready, honey! Today's the day!"". ""Okay! I'll be right out!"" I instinctively yelled back. I headed out of bed and noticed that I was fully clothed already like I had prepared to leave the night before. I also felt very spry but disregarded that thought. I headed towards the dining room to meet and eat my breakfast. ""You're late, hurry up and eat breakfast!"". ""Sorry, mom, I guess I overslept,"" I said that instinctively too. I looked at the time, and it was 10:30 am, and anxiety welled up inside me. I looked down at the crispy bacon and eggs my mother had served me, and a tear rolled down my cheek, knowing that this would be the last time I would eat this dish for a long time. Knowing the time, I quickly inhaled it and made my way outside to my car, where my dad was waiting. ""Hey kiddo, I packed all of your stuff in your car; You're good to go."" ""Thanks, Dad,"" I replied, giving him a long hug while my mother rushed outside to join us. ""Do good out there, son."" said my dad as I made my way to my car.

""I will."" With that, I set off on my three-hour journey to the college I would be attending. The thought of me finally moving out and going to college was elating. I had applied for so many scholarships and met so many people who helped me during my high school years. All of the hard work was finally paying off. I did not have to pay a dime for college since I had accumulated enough scholarships to pay for it. I formed relationships with many adults who helped teach me about college and the different tools to attend. I was appreciative of all of those positive influencers in my life. After a couple of long hours, I had finally made it to my new school and had moved into a dorm. I was exhausted from the drive so, I had decided to close my eyes for a bit.

I woke up to the smell of eggs and bacon. My eye slowly opened, and I was gazing at a beautiful woman standing over me, waving the eggs and bacon in my face. ""Wake up, honey."" said the woman. My eyes were fully open now. That's right, I work at Apple, I have my master's degree in photonics engineering, I have a beautiful wife, and a wonderful home. My wife picked up a piece of bacon, and I happily let her feed it to me. ""This is the life I've wanted to live,"" I whispered to myself. ""Your birthday is tomorrow; you'll be turning 46!"" she exclaimed, putting the plate of breakfast on my lap. ""Yeah, I don't look too old, do I?"" I replied while munching on another piece of bacon. ""You look more handsome every day,"" she said. I smiled, finishing my breakfast. After finishing my breakfast, I prepared myself for work, kissed my wife, and headed out the door. Looking back on my life made me appreciate myself for all of the hard work it took to get to this point. I hopped in my car and thought, ""today is going to be awesome,"" and I pulled out of the driveway and off to work.

Zemira

By Jacqueline Diehl (Finalist)

As a child I was told of the kingdom in the sky. It was a beautiful and magical place. Everyday I would wake up and hope I would be in the sky, looking over the sea that looks like glass. Each time when I would wake up in my own bedroom with the butterflies on the wall, I would cry for my parents because I was not in the kingdom in the sky. Looking back I realized how ridiculous it actually sounded. I am sixteen now and I forgot about the kingdom, until I was walking down the street with a couple friends. We were walking over a sewer drain and I saw a bright light shooting through the cracks, I bent down to look at it and I heard "Zemira".

Later that night I kept thinking about the name Zemira, I know I heard of it before, but I could not think of where I heard it from. Sitting on my bed I grabbed my laptop and looked up the name. Only one website popped up with that name, I closed my eyes and clicked on the link. I felt this strange sensation in my head and when I opened my eyes I was no longer in my room. Instead of my big blue bed, there were pink fluffy clouds that reminded me of cotton candy. I turned around and there was the sea of glass, that I have longed to see for so long. There was a sunset that was reflected through the water, I started to take a step forward to stick my hand into the water, when the call of a trumpet stopped me.

I heard the heavy sound of their footsteps as they came near, I instinctively put my hands above my head and turned around. There before me was the most beautiful white horse where a boy with shiny armor was seated. "Who are you and what is your business here?" he said with his voice echoing around me. "I...um I am Amelia," I choked out, still scared of his presence. "Amelia! As in Amelia Grace?" he asked with surprise taking. "Uh, yes" I said, surprised he knew my name. "Come with me!" he said smiling and stretching his hand down to me. I cautiously stretched my hand up to his. His hand engulfed mine and pulled me up behind him on top of the beautiful white horse. He clicked his tongue and the horse took off quickly, I was startled how fast it was moving and almost fell, until the knight grabbed my arm and wrapped it around his waist.

"What is your name?" I yelled over the sound of the thundering hoofs of the horses. "It's Charles" he shouted back. Very knightly I thought to myself and giggled. I was just about to ask where we were heading when a beautiful blue and gold castle appeared in the clouds. I gasped, This couldn't be the kingdom in the sky could it? "How are we supposed to get up there?" I asked. Charles looked over his shoulder and gave me a sly smile, I was confused until I felt myself floating. I looked down over the side of the horse, noticing the wings that have magically appeared from nowhere. I tightened my grip around Charles' waist and I didn't loosen it until we were safely back on the ground.

"What is this place?" I asked, jumping down from the horse and spinning trying to look at everything. "You don't know what this place is?" I shook my head. "It's Zemira, and you are the princess!" he said grabbing my hand and pulling me towards the castle. So, Zemira was a real place, unless this was a dream. I pinched myself quickly but I was still in the same place. "No I possibly can't be a princess...wait if I am a princess then that means my mom is the queen!" "Well actually, your parents are the king and queen!" "Wait, parents?" "Yes, your parents," he said almost as confused as I was. My dad died when I was super young and I never knew him. Maybe this will be my chance to actually get to know him. I got really excited and when Charles went to grab my hand again to lead me to the castle, I was basically dragging him.

Charles led me to a grand room with a tall ceiling and gold trim. As we started walking down the beautiful rug, I noticed the two people in the middle of the room, sitting in golden and red chairs. "Do I need to bow?" I asked nervously. Charles just chuckled, shaking his head at me and continued leading me towards my parents. "Amelia, is that you?" the woman dressed in a beautiful gown said with my moms voice. "Yes," I said, my voice sounding more confident then I felt. The woman came running towards me and pulled me into a huge hug. I hugged her back and when I looked for her shoulder I saw the man come toward us with tears in his eyes. I pulled away from my mom and ran to my dad, I threw myself at him. I cried with him.

We sat holding each other and crying for what seemed like forever, until one of the servants came saying dinner was ready. We all headed to the dining room, which was as beautiful to the rest of the house. We talked through the whole dinner and there was a lot laughing and crying. After dinner we headed to a seating room, where we continued until it got really late and we went to bed with promises to continue our conversation and to spend some quality time to catch up and get to know each other tomorrow.

100 Mile Journey

By Jonathan Eisert (Finalist)

I truly believe I am the only one in the world who notices the absurdities around here-

Ever since I could remember, even when I was a child, it seems I am the only sane one here. The people here act like they don't see anything that happens on a day-to-day basis. However, none act as bad as my roommate: Marcus.

"Hey! You ready to leave yet?"

Speak of the devil.

Marcus and I have been living together for the last couple of years; it's actually a great deal since I get to laze off of him. Besides the point, this is a great time to show what I mean about how weird it is here.

We decided to just walk to the store as the weather is great, and we haven't been on a walk recently. Speaking of the store we are going to. I don't actually know the name, but it has everything you could ever want: toys to spend the day with, snacks for when you're hungry, clothes for when you want to dress out, and most importantly, this is the local hangout spot, so you always get to meet someone new. The both of us finished getting dressed and left the house.

Right off the rip, the crazies showed up, once we stepped outside the neighbors were screaming.

"Where are my cashews Sandra!" screamed Sandra's husband. "I didn't eat your nut's john! And for the last time, they are nuts. Not cashews!"

This is what I have to deal with every time I come outside. If it isn't about their food, they are screaming at me calling me names. The problem is that I try to tell them to shut up, or I'll defend my honor when they try to bully me, and somehow I'm the bad guy! Marcus acts like our neighbors don't have it out for me, and just tells me to shut up. I decided to not let it worry me today, and we continue our journey.

Not long after we pass them we come upon the next mystery: the enchanted forest. At least that is what I have come to call it, once you walk past a certain point daytime vanishes, and night takes over. Marcus as usual doesn't seem to notice or care for that matter. However, I care! I won't let this mystery go undocumented. I try and take samples or note the unnatural sounds, and smells, but just like before my intentions don't reach Marcus. Marcus doesn't mind this area as much as I and after looking at what I'm doing for a moment, he continues on.

You might have noticed by now-- Marcus and I don't talk much on our walks. It isn't because we are mad at each other or anything like that. He just enjoys listening to music while I enjoy listening to the world-- even if it is full of crazies.

Finally, we have exited the mystical 40-second forest, but it felt like an eternity to me! I don't mention it to Marcus, but I hate this part of the walk. I don't want him to think I'm weak, or a scaredy cat, because I'm not! However, this part is constantly full of freaks and monsters. Beings that can touch the sky, lifeforms that move faster than light, and an impossibly slim walkway that one misstep will mean certain death.

Starting from the easiest to deal with, to the worst: the 10ft beings. Honestly, the only reason they aren't that hard to deal with is that they appear in more places than just here. Actually, they have been around for all my life, none seem to mind them, so I try my hardest to not worry much, but some carry the air of a monster. I mainly stare straight down and try to mind my business, but then the next obstacle comes in my way: the impossibly fast lifeforms.

I'm pretty sure they aren't actually alive, but they seem more like sentient robots than anything else. These robots work together with the previously mentioned beings with a weird relationship. The robots eat said beings but will bring them wherever they want. After this, they spit them out and wait to continue the cycle. What hasn't been mentioned is the speed these robots move at, it has to be at least a million miles an hour? A few times they have instigated me, so I obviously retaliate trying to fight them, but they always run away! I have to chase after them to carry on the fight, but Marcus, like with our neighbors, gets mad at me; he doesn't even care that the other started it.

After all this, lastly, we come to the walkway. Honestly, it doesn't take long to pass, but it has to be the scariest. This is because you have to walk on a small pathway across a 30-foot area of pure blackness. If you step off of this path you can almost certainly be hit by one of these robots mentioned above which is the terrifying part--Trust me, I've seen it firsthand. Aha! We have passed the last hurdle of our journey.

Marcus has to be a warrior of some kind. This is the only reasoning that makes sense for how he acts so nonchalantly through all these events.

Through thick-and-thin, our journey has almost come to an end. All that is left for me and Marcus is a minute-or-two long walk with no real worries along the way. My excitement is starting to bubble over as the anticipation starts to build. This is the reason I make this journey every time. There is no other place that makes me feel this way.

"Are you ready Alfred?" Marcus asked. He finally took his headphones out, so he could pay attention

"Ready!" I screamed at him.

""Ready!"" "Rea-oof!" "woof!"" I chanted while walking into the store.

My tail wagging the whole time as Marcus and I finally entered the Pet Store.

Pumpkin

By Mia Schramm (Finalist)

Long ago, there was an urban legend about a boy named
Pumpkin. He wasn't any ordinary boy, he had the ability to
grant people one wish every November 1st. Legend says if you
wished for something pure, you'd be gifted with an eternal life.
But, if you wished for selfish treasures then you'd no longer be
able to speak. Your voice would cost you your deepest desires. I
had read about this legend in the ancient section in our high
school's library, but didn't believe it was possible. Besides, what
would I wish for? I had already lost both my parents in a car
accident. I was learning to cope with their deaths, and visited
them daily. I would walk to school early to ensure I had enough
time to talk to them, even if they could never hear me. Today, I
knew it was going to be a difficult day for me. The one year
anniversary of their deaths. The day replayed in my head
millions of times, even occurred in nightmares. Each dream
more vividly descriptive than the last. I was nearly at the
cemetery, when I heard a twig snap behind me. A boy, about
my age steps out from a random tombstone, "I'm sorry, I didn't

mean to make noise. I just didn't want anyone to see me visiting". I took particular notice of his face, the way his jaw was perfectly crafted, the boldness he gave off as he spoke, and his eyes as blue as the ocean itself. I spoke softly, "It's alright. I don't mind, I was just coming to visit my parents".

He frowns, "You've lost someone"? I smile, feeling a sneaky tear slip down my cheek. "Yes. Last year actually. I lost both of my parents to a car accident. I-I never got to tell them bye". He approaches me, "Oh. I'm sorry. I shouldn't have asked-". I smile, blinking away the tears, "It's alright. I've just never talked to anyone about it. I usually keep this to myself". He interrupts me, "Because you're afraid to let people in"? I nod, and he pulls me into an unexpected hug. I accept the affection, losing myself in his touch. He just holds me. I relax at his touch, and his embrace as I feel tears slipping down my face. I pull away for a second, and he touches my hand. "What's one thing you would wish for right now"? I smile at him, "I want nothing more than love". He grins, "That's the purest answer I've ever heard. I will grant you your wish". I gasp, "But, that's impossible. No one can grant wishes, unless they're the great Pumpkin. That would have to mean. The legend? You're Pumpkin"?

He smiles, and laughs. "Most folks call me Jack nowadays, but yes the legend is true. However, there's a prophecy of a girl who'd visit her dead loved ones on this day, but only wish for love. She'd be the end of my curse, but a beginning of the purest of all loves". I smiled, "So, you were cursed? I'm the prophecy"? He nods, "I was cursed to grant wishes eternally because of something I did in my youth. The gods decided this would be a worthy punishment. However, a wise old woman told me of this prophecy, and I started counting the years. Praying each year to come, things would be different. The results were the same until today that is'. I took his hand, "Does this mean you're free of your curse"? He smiles, "That's exactly what it means". After that, he walked with me to drop off flowers to my parents. The rest of the day we spent getting to know each other, turns out we had a lot more in common than I thought. He is the greatest love in my life now, and for that I'm grateful for the foretold prophecy.

SECTION 4 – SUSPENSE

The Alley

By Harrison Keeler (Finalist)

The consistent pitter-patter of water droplets landing on the concrete echoed down the long alleyway and sent chills through Tom's body. The clouds obscured almost all light from the moon, and any light the clouds didn't block out, the tall ominous buildings surrounding them did.

"You know, I don't see the point in doing this. What are we trying to prove anyway?" Tom tried to argue.

"It's not what we're trying to prove. It's what you have to prove," George whispered back. Tom sighed, and they kept walking towards the next corner in the alley. As they neared the bend, something behind them clanged onto the concrete and sent Tom jumping into the air. They turned around just in time to see the silhouette of something leaping into the shadows.

"What was that?" Tom's eyes widened with fear.

"Probably just a cat or something. Let's keep moving." George replied almost too calmly. As they continued on, Tom couldn't help but think that it had been something other than a cat that they had heard behind them. He pushed the thought to the back of his mind.

As they rounded the next turn, their eyes locked on to a flickering light at the end of the alley, bobbing slowly up and down. Tom froze mid-step, his breath caught in his throat by fear of what they saw now. The hair on the back of his neck was suddenly sticking straight up. The light stood still for a moment and seemed to fly straight towards them. They jumped behind a barrel, and the light went out instantly. Tom didn't move. He sat there for what felt like an hour, a million things racing through his head. What was that? What am I doing here? He glanced at George who looked to be just as frightened as he was.

"Think it's gone?" George asked at barely a whisper.

"Maybe, look around the barrel and see if it's still there," answered Tom in the same tone of voice. George peered around the barrel and saw nothing but the dark alley. He gestured for Tom to stand up with him. Then, out of nowhere, George started sprinting towards the next corner. Tom followed, but still a few steps behind because of the sudden start. George stopped just around the corner, and Tom came up to stand next to him.

"This is it," George said, fear obvious in his voice. "This is Dead Men Alley."

Tom's eyes widened the name. "Why would a street be called 'Dead Men Alley'?"

"It's called Dead Men Alley because many years ago, on this very night, a group of three factory workers were walking home when they were attacked. The next morning their bodies were found mutilated and hanging from the wall. To this day, the mystery of who or what killed them has never been solved. Their ghosts roam this street each year on the night of their death, searching for revenge." George explained with a serious look on his face.

Tom looked at him, concern written all over his face. Then he took a breath and tried to relax. "Whatever," he exhaled. "You probably just got that from a stupid movie or something."

"Alright, think what you will, but all you have to do is walk down this street alone to pass the test," George replied. Tom glanced down the street for only a second, then looked back to where George had been to ask, "What test?" Except, George was gone.

Tom then heard a voice say, "See you on the other side." Tom was left alone in this haunted alley. Beads of sweat began to drip down his face. I could just run back the way we came and end this now, he thought. Except if he did that, everyone at school would think he was afraid of some street. No, he would do it, he had to. He took one step into the alley, and a brick smashed onto the ground in front of him. He leaped backward in fright, a small yelp escaping his mouth. Just a brick, he thought, nothing more. He regrouped and started to walk down the street once more. This time a piece of metal clanged to the ground; he kept walking.

"Think you're brave do you, trying to walk across our alley uninvited?" A voice boomed out of the darkness and an eerie laugh echoed down the alley. Tom covered his ears, put his head down, and ran. He ran as fast as he could towards the far end of the alley, ignoring any noise that his hands didn't block out. He made it to the end and put his hands on his knees, gasping for air. He stood up and looked back down the alley and saw nothing. Then the feeling that he was being watched crept into his mind. He spun around, searching in every direction.

All of a sudden bright lights illuminated the alley, surrounding him in a blinding light.

"Congratulations, you've passed the test. Welcome to the Chess Club."

Flesh of Sin

By Elijah (Finalist)

"Have you ever questioned what causes humans to commit acts of evil against each other? You know what I'm talking about right? You know….the usual stuff. Things like murder, rape, manipulation, enslaving….yeah, those things. Well, you still might not get an answer after this. That's because I've seen what enslaves humanity and causes us to commit such horrific acts against each other. It makes no sense. It's so bad that it makes me laugh. Not because it's funny, but because laughing takes me away from the horrors beyond what the mind can comprehend. Although, I should give you some context on how I found out my findings. It's not a lot, but I had someone killed the week before. I'm a businessman, I have money to make. She didn't like my strategies. She wanted to rat me out, man. You know what would happen if they found out my "secrets," right? I didn't feel bad about it for 5 days. On the 6th day, I started to feel a heaviness in my heart. As if I did something wrong. The 7th day is when I saw it. I woke up that day and started my morning routine as usual. It happened as I walked out of the door. The grotesque and horrific sight that laid before my eyes.

Everywhere I looked, masses of unknown flesh pulsated rhythmically, releasing a strange, black gas into the air. Several large, disgustingly shaped creatures with large eyes that covered their bodies hovered over the city, slowly moving as if they were watching over all the chaos that was happening below them. I saw couples walking together, being linked together by a gray, glue-like mass that had distorted, incomplete mouths on it. The mouths had tongues and tentacles that would caress all over their bodies and bring them closer together. Others had large boils on their bodies. Some of the boils exploded and released a strangely colored gas that sunk into the floor. Then, two guys bumped into each other. It was then I figured out what was going on. The gas rushed up to their noses, as if it were alive, and made the two argue with each other. It escalated quickly into a fight, that for some reason, led to one of them dying. The one still standing had blood on him. He started to turn into this horrific monster as he ran away from the scene. He hid in a dark alley before I could witness the full transformation. It was at that moment that I also saw something else that was strange. There was someone who was seemingly unaffected by all of this. No boils, no masses of flesh, nothing. She watched the scene in horror. As if what she was seeing was any more terrifying than what I saw that day. She was carrying some sort of book in her hand. I pinched myself, slapped my cheek, and rubbed my eyes just to check if I was dreaming. Of course....It was no dream. It was all real. It was hell. The moment I found myself questioning reality out of fear, the creatures in the sky were all looking at me. They were gazing into my soul. Piercing my heart with their cosmic gaze. I could've sworn I heard one of them say, "You are already one of us." I couldn't do anything else but run back into my home and hide there. No food, no water, nothing for the rest of the day.

Actually, I'm getting ready to kill myself. No way in hell I'm gonna witness that again. Oh yeah….the Bible. Haha….what God would allow this to happen? Unless…."

Crimson Winter

By Asa Handy (Finalist)

"Elizabeth, hurry up!"

"James, I'm going as fast as I can!"

It had been a rough few months for these two. For as long as they could remember, their marriage had been basically perfect. Granted, they had their share of tiffs now and again, but they always managed to make up. That is until the twins left. The older of the two, Seth, was a mamma's boy, always by her side, laughing and bright. Cassandra, on the other hand, was her dad's favorite. Still, they all loved each other very much.

Things were never the same after they moved out. Little incidents, the kind that would normally be forgiven, set them off. They couldn't handle it. They needed a change.

Having lived in Louisiana all their lives, both had never had the opportunity to see snow. After some research, they decided to go to a cabin in Colorado Springs. So, with their bags in the trunk, they started the 14-hour drive from Shreveport, Louisiana.

The drive over was a quiet one. Mr. Beauchamp did most of the driving. Mrs. Beauchamp passed the time by looking out the window, occasionally commenting on the trees as they passed or a car she saw in the rear-view window.

"James, isn't that an oldy?" Mrs. Beauchamp exclaimed, pointing to a red Chevy Camero behind them.

"What a fun one. Haven't seen one of those in ages."

Mr. Beauchamp glanced out the rear-view mirror. "Looks like the other five cars you've pointed out. Now would you please give me some peace and quiet?"

Mrs. Beauchamp turned back toward the window. She felt tears welling up in her eyes. Seeing her children leave had been hard enough. She couldn't bear to lose her husband as well. She remained quiet, listening to the sound of the wind rushing past the car, steady and relaxing.

****

"We're here. Let's unpack." Mrs. Beauchamp awoke suddenly. The fresh scent of pine and the night wind heightened her senses. As she stepped out of the car, she felt the entirety of her shoe sink into 12 inches of lovely, white powder.

"Oh, James! Isn't this wonderful? I love how crisp the air feels." She paused.

"Has anyone else been here lately?"

"No."

"Why is the door open?"

Mr. Beauchamp let out a sigh. "I don't know. The owners just forgot to close it? Stop worrying, Elizabeth. Come on."

After many armloads of bags and suitcases, they were finally settled in. Mrs. Beauchamp let out a sigh as she sat down.

"Finally! We can relax. It's been so long since we've been able to get away."

James walked out of the kitchen, his brows furrowed. "Do you smell something?"

Mrs. Beauchamp paused a moment.

"No. Not that I…" She stopped, sniffing. "Actually, yes. What is that?"

"Could be the garbage." Mr. Beauchamp walked back to the kitchen. "Found it." He lifted up the trash bag, full to the brim.

"Nasty! Get that out of here!"

Tying it off, Mr. Beauchamp left. A few minutes passed.

"My stars. Where is that man?" She shook her head.

Standing up, she walked to the bedroom to lie down. The door was locked. Strange. She walked back to the living room. Grabbing the keys the owners had left them, she walked back to the door and unlocked it.

The first thing to hit her was the smell, hot and moist. She stumbled back, gagging.

"James!"

She felt a tingle of fear run through her. She slowly walked to the bed. Crouching down, Mrs. Beauchamp lifted the bed skirt. She froze. The owner's eyes, gray and lifeless, stared back into hers. She could only think of one thing... Run!

Mrs. Beauchamp scrambled to her feet, sprinting toward the door. She slammed into it. It wouldn't open. It wouldn't open!

She fumbled for the keys. Bedroom, shed, windows. Front door! She shoved the key into the lock.

Suddenly, darkness. Mrs. Beauchamp listened. Silence. The generator had been cut. She needed to find James. She twisted the key as hard as she could. The door flew open.

Snow was falling from the night sky, covering everything - the red car! She recognized that car. Where was James?

"James!"

As if on cue, he appeared. He was clutching his arm, bruises visible under his fingers. The gash in his head dripped along his cheekbone, finding its way down his chin.

"Oh, James! What happen..."

"Get in the car. Now!" Mr. Beauchamp grabbed her hand. They sprinted toward the car, breathing heavily in the cold air. They reached the car, climbing in quickly.

"Where are the keys?"

"What?"

"Elizabeth, where are the keys?!" She fell silent. Mr. Beauchamp's gaze followed hers. Fifty feet away, under the stillness of the night, the keys rested in the freshly fallen snow.

"Stay here." As her husband left, Mrs. Beauchamp felt the hairs on the back of her neck stand up.

"James?"

She suddenly heard the sound of fists hitting the rearview window. She stiffened. She wanted to look. She couldn't look. She knew what she'd see.

The driver's door suddenly closed. Mr. Beauchamp plunged the key into the ignition.

"Hold on." Shifting into gear, he floored the pedal as hard as he could. Mrs. Beauchamp stared behind her, watching as the silhouette of a man, a knife in one hand, faded into the distance.

The Murk

By Cheyanna Xenos (Finalist)

Being alone and feeling alone are two different things. I always imagined being alone would be worse but I soon found out that being surrounded by people who can't hear you scream is just as bad.

I always felt out of place. Like I was a spare screw on a cheap bookshelf. I might be useful for something else but most of the time I am forgotten and thrown away. I didn't mind it though and honestly never thought twice about it. But yesterday on my way home from school I felt my stomach drop and the need to catch myself, even though I wasn't falling. The world looked distorted but it only lasted for a few seconds. I did my best to shake the feeling on my way home. I tried to work out how I would explain the feeling to my mom, knowing I would end up keeping it to myself like I always did.

I made it to my driveway the same time my mom pulled in. I waved but she was too busy on the phone to notice. She opened the door and I slipped in before it shut completely and made my way to my room. I felt the feeling again but this time I noticed the world seemed out of focus. I could feel my heartbeat pounding as I ran down the hall to the living room. I watched as my dad walked but I couldn't hear the door close, I could see his mouth moving but the words were muffled by a ringing in my ear.

I finally could make out the words "Hey where's Jadan?" as my dad yelled out to my mom in the kitchen. I couldn't hear her response the look on her face made it clear she had not seen me either.

"Maybe he stayed after school" I hear my dad say. I try hard to hear my mom's side of the conversation but the more I try the louder my heartbeat gets.

"I'm right here." I try to say, hoping that if they could hear me I would be able to get rid of the awful feeling. Still, no one acknowledged me. I ran right up to my dad giving him one last look, just hoping that maybe, just maybe he would see me. My heart broke as I looked through me as if I wasn't even there.

I walked down the street trying everything in my power to wake myself up. The feeling was getting stronger, the feeling of falling and floating at the same time. I couldn't help myself and neither could an else, I was alone, surrounded by hundreds of people.

I gave in and embraced the sinking feeling, knowing there was nothing that I could do to stop it, and this time instead of sinking I felt a hand wrap around my arm. And whatever was pulling me under let go of me losing the battle to the stranger.

"Hello! I am glad to see you made it through the Murk." came a female voice. I opened my eyes but quickly closed them due to how bright it had gotten. I felt glasses slide on my ears and her voice brush past my ears again. How amazing it felt to hear audible words again.

"Sorry about that you can open your eyes again," she said. I followed her directions, even though the context of this whole situation didn't sit with me right. The lady gave me a smile as she handed me a cup of water.

"Hi Kane," she said, looking rather unsure of herself. I was confused but I took the water anyway not sure if correcting her was in my best interest. She got up and walked over to a desk opening a folder before turning around in pure shock. Her elbow slipped off the counter as she frantically put herself together again

"You are Kane, right?" she said behind frantic laughter "otherwise we are both in trouble". Realizing she too couldn't get in trouble I felt I should be honest. "...eh, not exactly..my name is Jadan"

Drinking and Driving

By Yoset Reyes (Finalist)

Although, there are many policies in place to advocate against drunk driving, there are those who would endanger themselves and others with their thoughtless actions when they jump into the driver's seat of a car. The average first DUI has fines around $500, with a jail sentence of 3 days or going to drinking and driving classes, and losing their license from six months to a year. Any further DUI convictions result in higher and higher fines, restrictions, and punishment. The biggest punishment comes from vehicular manslaughter. This is a felony and will give you prison time, usually between twenty years and life depending on the person's previous record. Driving drunk and being convicted more than four times in many states changes the charge from a misdemeanor to a felony, which impacts jobs and even includes prison time. These are some very big incentives to not drink and drive.

Drinking and driving under the influence refers to being behind the wheel of a car while drunk. This is considered the single biggest cause of road carnage today. It is illegal in almost all countries of the world to not only drive but also operate any machinery while under the influence of alcohol. The main reason is alcohol usually impairs one's judgment thereby making one unfit to operate a machine or drive. When out on a drinking spree, you should always have a designated drive to ensure you reach home in one piece. Excessive consumption of alcohol has many causes. Most youths that are victims of driving while drunk usually do it trying to impress their friends. Psychologists have also established a link between excessive drinking in young people with the need for attention. Most young people do this as a way of seeking the attention of their parents who are too busy to notice them. Among adults, use of other drugs is cited as one of the leading causes to excessive alcohol consumption. A mixture of drugs in ones systems easily impairs ones judgment and most people end up drinking too much without even realizing it. Whenever you have taken too much alcohol, the functioning of your brain is impaired which results in poor judgment. These usually result in unnecessary risk taking. What usually happens is the brain takes more time to execute on some cognitive functions that require lightning fast responses. Information is therefore processed slower when you are drunk as opposed to when you are sober. Alcohol actually reduces the cognitive function of the brain by up to 30%.

This explains why a drunk driver doesn't see very far. In addition to this, alcohol consumption also leads to blurred and double vision. Driving when you are not seeing properly is nothing short of an accident waiting to happen. A drunk person is also overconfident which is the main reason that drunk people characteristically take unnecessary risks. Research shows that younger people are at greater risk than older people. This is because older people have probably been drinking for years and have a great alcohol tolerance unlike the younger ones who are probably just starting out. However, most young people move in packs and often use cabs so only 10% of the accidents that happen due to drunk drivers are caused by drives below 21 years of age. But there is also the issue of underage drinking and driving. It raises the question of how the underage alcohol abusers access the alcohol to begin with. While some use fake ids to buy drinks, others easily access alcohol at home. Still, there are some unscrupulous businessmen who turn the other way and allow underage clients to purchase alcoholic drinks from them.

The use of breathalyzers, introduction of government sponsored campaigns, and punitive measures should be used to try to curb drunk driving. Such steps will reduce the wanton loss of life and property due to the numerous accidents that have been attributed to driving while drunk.

Sin Island

By Caeden Conklin (Finalist)

Thud! A man named Victor Hill was thrown against the sandy beach with a burlap bag on his head and his arms and feet chained up. The island he was on was only known by a few and named Sin Island. Victor was a leader of a vicious gang, that maliciously killed 30 innocent civilians in the past year during their bank robberies, drive-by shootings, and while defending their territory.

A man with a deep voice yelled, "This is Sin Island! The only way to make it off the island is by getting to the center and confronting your past mistakes. You will soon learn exactly what I mean." After the mysterious man was done speaking his piece, Victor felt someone removing his chains. As all this was happening, Victor remained calm. He was smarter than most and knew panicking would only make things worse. Once he was free from the heavy chains, he slowly removed the bag from his head and stood up. He cautiously looked around at his surroundings. The island appeared to be constructed of a densely packed jungle. Victor looked behind him to try and see the man who imprisoned him, but all he could see was a boat sailing off into the horizon. As Victor examined his surroundings, trying to figure out what to do, he noticed a large backpack had been placed at his feet. Inside the backpack there was a knife, rope, fire starter, water purifier, sleeping bag, and a note which stated:

This island is filled with many natural resources, you should have no problem finding food, water, and items to build a shelter. What you need to worry about are your past mistakes. They will haunt you more and more as you move further into the heart of the island, they may even kill you. The only way to guarantee your survival is to reach the center of the island. There you will meet a group of spiritual leaders that will determine if you are worthy of going back home. If you are, you will be guided back to the shore where a boat, with navigation equipment, will be waiting for you. If not, you have not fully confronted your sins and need to continue searching the island.

Victor put the note back in his backpack and started to walk along the edge of the jungle looking for any food he could take with him. He also wanted to see just how large the island was. After what seemed to be hours, Victor stopped his search and determined it would get him nowhere. He went into the jungle to look for supplies so that he could build a campfire for the night. Victor found many fruits as well as dried leaves and twigs to use for the fire.

Once Victor set up camp for the night he sat down to eat. He reached into the backpack where he was storing the fruit, but there was nothing there. Looking at the backpack more closely, he found no holes that the fruit would have fallen out of. As he was trying to figure out what had happened, he heard something chewing a juicy piece of fruit across from him, on the other side of the fire. He grabbed his knife from the bag and quickly turned to see what was across from him. It was a small boy about middle school age, who had a familiar face.

"Give me back my food," Victor said with a slight hint of anger in his voice.

"No," responded the boy.

Surprised by how tranquil the child was, Victor raised his knife, "I will only say this one more time, give me back my food."

The boy simply repeated, "No."

Even though Victor was normally able to remain calm and assess a situation, the island had started to mess with his mind. He did not know it yet, but he would eventually start to feel the panic his victims and their families experienced when he harmed them. He walked over to the boy and raised his knife to intimidate him. But the boy simply said, "I would not do that if I were you. You used to steal Bobby Clark's lunch almost every day in 6th grade and you must experience his pain."

As soon as the boy said the name Bobby Clark, Victor realized why the face looked so familiar. The boy looked exactly like Bobby, the boy he used to bully in middle school. But in Victor's mind, it was impossible for an island to know his past and that this was just his mind playing tricks on him. Enraged by his food being stolen, he cut the boy on his arm. As he did so, pain shot down his own arm in the same spot he cut the boy.

Still in a calm voice, the boy stated, "Continuing to cause pain will not solve your problems. That is the exact reason you were brought to this island."

As Victor's hunger grew and the island's grip on his mind increased, he started to panic. He wanted to hurt the boy and just take the fruit he gathered himself but knew that would not work. He turned and started to walk back to the jungle to gather more fruit. As he faced the jungle, he noticed mysterious figures moving around, but could not tell what they were until he took a few more steps. The figures appeared to be people he had traumatized. Filled with fear, he stopped walking and stood still. The boy that looked like Bobby walked in front of him and said, "Many people would have no problem getting off this island. But you..." he took a long pause to look behind him. He then looked back at Victor and continued, "But you clearly hurt too many people to make it out of here alive."

Before Victor could say anything, the people surrounded him. Victor then spoke his final words, "Forgive me."

The Deal

By Cliff Fraley (Finalist)

I grew up in Latintown, the part of the Franks where the entire district was run by Latin Americans, primarily by the gangs and cartels who called it home. I was born from a local legend, Yara Venganza, former member of the Solo Madres who went after a child slave ring when I was only a month old. My older brother I never knew was kidnapped and bought by some corp executive in Dayton, and died there a sex slave. According to the other mothers there, she had him castrated and nailed to an undercross. She never spoke of it around me when she came back home, but it was her demeanor that told me everything, and it was knowing that's the life I may have no choice but to live in is what hardened me.

Mama always kept me in eyesight, alongside my three younger brothers. Only time I wasn't allowed out of her sight was when I had to use the bathroom, even then we all knew she had her ear perched against the door. Always allowed to go out, only when I knew to run back should anyone start eyeing me, but mostly we never went out alone as she always persisted we go with her to go see a play or Tommy Redhand, a local street performer who could strum a guitar faster than a machine gun spat out bullets. She never let us go any other place, and she was right to do so as a mother. Should she allow us to go with our friends wherever they pleased, I may have ended up a junkie or street scraper early on.

Despite mama's carefulness and due diligence, we all found a way to worm ourselves out of her sight. First day I toured the streets was the first day I cut school. They never reached out to my mother, the teacher's didn't care about me or any student who wasn't progressing. After jumping the play yard fence and taking a back alley to Seventh Steel Boulevard, me and a friend named Chino walked to his brother's apartment a few minutes walk away, nestled in the rundown Secte complex. When we got there, his older brother Luise was tinkering with some street grade tech, using it to make a tec shotgun. First time I ever saw a gun that day, all at age 12. The peculiar part was when he handed it to Chino, and when they both looked at me.

"Hey, Sebastian, wanna do a gun run with us?" Said Chino. Those words are forever scarred in my memory. Like a scared kid wanting to oppress his emotions, of course I said yes. Chino grinned, then grabbed the gun, which was two thirds his size, and wrapped it into a black blanket. We then left the house and walked to Creeger, a small little tower block dominated by the Hatians. When we arrived we were given stares. Felt like everyone was looking at me, even when I was behind them, like there were eyes on every part of their head. Gold plated arms and teeth, blacked out or glowing blue eyes, all signs of a Baron ganger. Never had to be outside to know them, mama told me all I needed about the gangs, always the bad about them. She told me the only things they cared about were their own and their Loa. They were prone to xenophobia, and seeing a lighter skin tone and a vato accent was greeted with skepticism.

We arrived at a apartment on the 15th floor, with the word's "fuck offff" graffittied in red all caps. A circular face with x's for eyes and a frown; Bad sign all the way. Chino never cared, never cracked his cool, and simply knocked on the door with the concealed gun. It immediately opens to the sight of a thug with a Baron Samedi mask on.

"Who de fuck are you, youngblood?" He asks in a deep and thick Hatian accent. Chino looks at him with emotionless eyes. "We're gift givers." He said with a cool demeanor. The Haitian steps backwards and to the side, allowing us to walk in. We wasted no time walking into the red room apartment, setting our sights on the black metal crow skulls mounted on the walls, with red glow stones illuminating as its eyes. Loa signs and the Baron insignia were spray painted all across the walls and ceilings, even on the screen of an old pre-war television. At that time I was afraid and curious why this sign was everywhere. Now I know people who spray and place the insignia everywhere are Voodoo possyboys, the kind that kill when crossed the wrong way.

The room was filled with clutter, dirty dishes, food trays, and people. Seven in total excluding us, all Hatians. Bioluminescent tattoos, augmented VR eyewear that glowed red. They all sat around taking whiffs of hyperpods, filled with Bliss to have them sit there and see the world go by, their minds in an active stasis. A closet's worth of weapons were scattered around the place; A hatchet was buried in a metal skull, nailed bats put up against the wall, knives sheathed in pant pockets, and pre-war guns tied to their waists. All bad signs. Chino kept his cool, eyes keen with perception. The Haitian had us walk through the main living room where the gun toters crashed high off Bliss, moving to the leftmost part where a set of two chairs were. He was the first to get there and plop himself on the chair, Chino was second. I stood behind him, looking around the room with my heart pounding.

"What is it Luise brought me today?" asked the Haitian. Chino replied by holding onto the loose end of the blanket and had the gun roll out of it, catching the gun by the barrel when it came loose, then handed it to the Haitian. When he took hold he was immediately impressed, with a smile showing his glowing garnet teeth. He began to caress the trigger button, analyzing the power nodes aligning the barrel's sides and looking into the amplification. Chico saw this and decided to speak.

"Each node gives it twenty amps, increasing the velocity and shock power." He spoke with confidence, and he was right. Thinking back, few would be as honest as Chino and Luise, as everyone else were big into upselling their designs. The Haitian looked to him, his smile now faded,replaced with a look of awe and disappointment. "So, with that being said, 20k." Said Chico with his hand held out. It was at that point things had gone south, as the Haitian scowled and stood up from his seat.

"You think you can fuck me? You, above all people, youngblood?" Screamed the Haitian. While I was beginning to panic and the other guys there began to get up and unsheath their knives, Chino still kept his cool, staring back at him, mouth closed. We were surrounded on all sides, one of them I keenly remember had a holo-face, and tuned it to the face of a Baron. He grabbed one of the spiked bats from the wall, another pulled the hatchet from the TV, and the dealer had the shotgun pointed at Chino with intent to kill written all over his face. Didn't matter to him, probably killed a kid or two prior. All of the sudden Chino smiled, even chuckled. I'm hearing this with wonder, in fact, it fueled me to abandon my fears, which I soon did.

"Oh yeah? Go on ahead, blast me loco Haitian." With those words coming from his mouth with a smooth cool to it I knew he'd be blown to a blood spray. The Haitian pulled the trigger on him a second after, and I closed my eyes to limit the gore I'd see. Indeed there was a blast, a loud one, the sound of a bomb going off. My ears rang, and no matter what I kept my eyes closed. However, when my ears came to, I heard Chino's voice, and he was laughing. Meanwhile the Haitian was screaming at the top of his lungs. I opened my eyes to a splatter of blood all over the walls, the other Haitians all stepped back a few feet, and the Haitian we dealt with rolling on the floor, hands missing. Instead bone, flesh and blood was there, exposed and gushing everywhere.

Without hesitation Chino pulled from his waist a one-day-use pop pistol, and pointed it on the nearest Haitian. He grabbed another one hidden in his ankle boot and tossed it to me. I was nervous, and with embarrassment then and even now, it slipped from my hands and fell on the floor. Virgin to violence at the time, but I was quick to pick it up and point it at them, darting from person to person. Chino I guess like my sporadic style, and began smirking. He kept his eyes keen on the opposition, then began speaking to me in Spanish.

"Sebastian, look at every single one of these bitches. If they even move, pop them, understand?" Didn't need to look at him to answer. I just nodded my head as I aimed down the sights of my pistol. He was the first to walk forward, the Haitian with his hands blown off threatening us, telling the other's to skewer us in his native tongue. With that gun in my hand I felt safe; all the fear was drained from my body. It was like nothing I'd ever before experienced, never before enjoyed. The fire in my chest burned away all fears, and when Chico got to the door, poked his head out and checked in case of reinforcements, then looked to me and waved the hand he held his gun in towards his vicinity. I kept my gun on each and every one of them, Chico included. We walked out without a scrape on us, and bolted out the block back to the Franks, back into Chino's house where we returned our guns, and then back to school.

We came back to the school ground in the middle of lunch, nobody asked questions. Every class we missed was giving us the stare, and that is where the fire faded. The fearlessness receded when that gun left my hand, and all day my hands were shaking. Only time I tried to suppress it was when madre arrived at school, coming to pick me up. When I got in her car I faked the usual day-to-day conversation we'd have. She'd ask como andas, I'd say estoy muy bien mamá. She'd ask if I'd learned anything, and in my head I wanted to tell her I learned I held a gun for the first time, nearly gotten killed for the first time, and was involved in a arms deal for the first time. Instead I told her I learned about the atomic sciences. At least it was the truth.

The day after we hit that deal, Chino came to me at school, asking me to come with him during the intermediate period of first and second block. He walked me to his locker, opened the door to it, then handed me a credchip with 5k on it. He told me then and there something that shocked me.

"The deal was meant to go south. When the puto's hands were blown off, the Solo Lobos nearby were tipped off that the guy who killed one of us was in there. Paid Luis and me, but I asked in a favor for you. Kept your name out the convo' though. Better for your sake cabron." After that he walked to the exit, once more skipping school. When I looked down onto that credchip, that same feeling experienced with that gun in my hand returned. Those two days I knew little of what it really was, until I realized it. That fire in my heart, that churning in my stomach, the adrenaline that pumped through me, it was pleasure. I began to enjoy it. I decided to go join him, and even had the balls to ask him a life changing question. "Chino, mind if I tag along in the next one?" All he did was smirk, and moved his head, meaning he wanted me to follow him.

6601

By Audrey Spillman (Finalist)

GROUND FLOOR

You are here. You are alone.

It's smaller on the inside, and for some reason, you can't remember unlocking the door or stepping inside. You can see just about every other room from any doorway on the first floor, but they're just far enough away from one another that you could not leap to the next room.

Silk rugs from every corner of the Earth soak the hardwood floors. The seas of rugs confuse you. There is red in every room and in every room where there is not red it's unbearably cold. You keep seeing the same set of furniture, but beside one another, they look as if from foreign collections. There are masks mounted on the walls, in the basement, and everywhere. There are tapestries for miles, rugs on walls... You could have sworn that your dream last night had you walking on those rugs on the walls, sideways... After a week, you're grateful for the cramped space. The floor plan is less confusing that way, though you still feel as though you're going in circles.

The fireplace won't light. You toss in a match, and in five minutes, it dies out again. You're so frustrated with it after some tries that you're tempted to get some gasoline and soak its wood and its white marble and its deeply coloured fake flowers, the black metal grate, the golden mirror above it, the trophy that sits atop it, the blue and red china... you want to watch it all burn.

A cat that is not yours appears where you cannot predict it. You saw it almost immediately when you drove up. It jumped into an evergreen bush, and turned into shadow. Now you see it every once and awhile. When you look up as you're eating dinner, it's sitting on the other side of the table across from you. It stares. You can feel it climb onto your stomach in the dead of night. You don't open your eyes.

It watches you. You've never caught it, never touched it. How long have you been here?

THE BASEMENT

You are here. You are alone.

But you once saw a man in a mask standing at the bottom of the stairs to the basement, on the landing. In front of a rug. The light's gone out. The mask, white and red. You can see no eyes behind the mask. The basement door only unlocks from the outside.

One day you go down into the basement to look around. Immediately to the side of the bottom of the stairwell, there is a covered doorway. A white tapestry keeps the room's secrets safe. Behind the tapestry, there is an abandoned study. Red rug on the floor. Records stacked forever on the shelves, books you've never seen before on every flat surface. Art you never bought. The favourite decoration of this room is blades. There are daggers on every shelf. Foreign daggers, glass knives, a miniature guillotine. Some blade that you can't put a name to. There's a display case, holding... a crocodile head.

The bookends are elephants. You look into their painted eyes. They are mad.

There is a door in this room that goes further into the ground. You'll never open that door in your life.

UPSTAIRS

You are here. You are alone.

Or are you?

The hall upstairs is open on one side, gaping down over the foyer. It offers the best view of the chandelier and the best surveillance of the front lawn. The master bedroom, without any outstanding features, has a room—the en-suite—off the side, which in turn has two rooms off its sides, a water closet and a walk-in. It also has a balcony, which overlooks the porch connected through a glass door to the kitchen downstairs. You choose not to sleep in the master. There are too many places for something to hide.

On the other end of the hall is a jack-and-jill bedroom and office, which both have a covered alcove in their walls and a hall with a closet and a sink and a bathroom and another sink room, and closet... doors cover doors cover doors. There are so many corners to turn in every room upstairs. The closet belonging to the bedroom has a laundry shoot. You grab at the cat just as it's jumping down into it, out of reach, out of sight.

You find the most mounted heads upstairs. There are mounted fish. More alligator skulls. In the jack and jill bedroom, there is a huge mounted boar. There are more masks, more mirrors, too much art to see through. More rugs. The walls in your room are deep red. There are two red rugs. Two red tapestries. Five calendars. Red curtains. Barely any light can get through to tell you when it is morning.

Though you never light incense, you always find it burning.

The man in a mask stands on the edge of your vision when you're tired. There are footsteps in the attic. Are they animal? The mounted heads look to you with spite. It seems they want a taste of revenge.

The masked man appears in your dreams. He stands too far to really see, but he is always watching you. The driveway is miles... you could never reach the end of it. When you go for walks, you encounter lake... after pond... after creek... after well... after lake... under the endless rain, the trees turn red.

The coyotes howl at night, loud and endless. There are deer in the yard on the peaceful days. They track you with their eyes.

The boar has been in your dreams lately. He smells your flesh. And he leaves again, climbing into the wall before you wake.

The black cat watches from a crack under a doorway. The masked man stands behind you. They only watch. They don't need to hurt you. They know you'll do yourself in.

You are here. You are not alone.

The Devil's Pawn

By Isabella Vasilides (Finalist)

They always say that one should never deal with the devil, but alas, some of us must play the part of the fool. I had no other choice; I needed an out. Excuses, of course, but nevertheless I used these thoughts as a way to justify my actions. In the end, there is truth to my claims.

As far as I can remember I've always been an orphan who was forced onto the cold, desolate streets. The life of a thief was the only fathomable future for me. There is no good fortune in the lives of tieflings. With wicked, curled horns, dark ebony eyes, and whip-like tails, we are a hellish sight to behold. We were the scum of society, treated worse than dogs. So, that is how I lived, diving from shadow to shadow, sunrise to sunset in an endless cycle. I would steal a crumb of bread here and a jug of water there. I did not relish this life, but it was all in the name of survival. Of course, as the years stretched on, I became more bitter of my situation, leading my habits to become more frivolous. Stealing shimmering gold trinkets with diamonds that sent light cascading against your skin, to fine silk fabrics carried by caravans from far off lands that felt as if you were wrapped in clouds themselves, why not indulge myself? After all, it wasn't my fault I was delt this ill-fated existence. I became a slave to greed, stealing from whomever and wherever I pleased. I even carved out a place for myself amongst the thieves of the land. There was no lock I couldn't pick and no guard I couldn't escape; until one day, when Icarus flew too close to the sun.

One day, word circulated to my ears of a cavern. A cavern that many men had foolishly wasted their lives trying to obtain the treasures which laid within its maw. The chasm itself wasn't cleverly hidden, nor was it heavily guarded. Instead, it was what settled within that incautious thieves lost their lives to. For this treasure trove was actually the lair of a slumbering demon. Being greed's pawn, I set out on my own doomed journey to claim the fool's gold. Under the cloak of midnight I wandered, following the map I had stolen from a drunkard at a tavern who had been gossiping about the fabled demon's riches. Through the cool night, with moonlight dancing off the branches of the whispering trees I trekked until I had finally reached it. Between the twisted trunks and gnarled roots of dark cedar trees laid a gapping abyss sloping downward. A soft light could barley be visible from deep within. It was too simple, the rational part of my brain said; but, regardless, I crept like a mouse into the lion's den.

Deeper and deeper the tunnel spiraled, branching off at multiple points, but I kept on a singular path as if a force was tugging me forward. Finally, I came to a room with dimly lit torches that made light dance off of the piles of gold and the plush velvet carpet. I ignored all of this, however, drawn instead to a small dagger sitting on an altar near the room's end. As soon as my fingertips brushed against its smooth golden hilt, I became paralyzed. The torches roared, casting light upon an imposing figure chained against the wall. The chains rattled as the being took a deep breath, and looked up at me with blindfolded eyes. A sick, twisted grin spread across its scared face, the ends of its mouth almost touching the tips of horns that curled around the creature's head.

Another fool has dared to pay me a visit. A deep, gravely voice vibrated within my skull. ""What is your name young one?""

Somehow, I was able to take a shaking breath and find my voice. "My name is Aris."

A shudder ran down my spine, and I felt as if the voice could see into my soul as it continued its speech."" My name is Seraph. Aris, I can see your past, and your future. You are on the path to ruin; death is upon you. You are a formidable thief with wasted potential. Unlike those who had come here before you; you can be saved. We have both been wronged in this world for reasons outside of our grasp. I offer you a preposition. Become my apprentice, I can offer you unimaginable power and a chance at new life. All I ask in return is for you to assist in my freedom. ""

A vision of myself surrounded by unknown people appeared before my eyes, but instead of people cursing and driving me away as usual, they were smiling and welcoming me with caring, loving arms. A flicker of warmth engulfed me but was snuffed out as swiftly as it came, leaving me as numb as before. Whoever this being was, they had the ability to peer into every crevice of my soul, revealing my deepest, most secret desire. A desire which I thought had died inside me many moons ago; the desire to be loved.

I dropped to my knees, knowing I was just handing my strings over to a new puppet master, but I've never had the strength to wield them on my own to begin with. My knuckles turned pale as they gripped the sheathed golden dagger, "I accept your offer, Seraph." And that is how I, the fool, became the devil's pawn.

Shattered

By Maddie Martin (Finalist)

"I am so sorry for your loss," the woman police officer whispered empathetically.

I couldn't respond. I sat there stunned and frozen in my seat, and my breaths were coming in short spurts. How could this happen? How could my best friend be dead?

My mother is now crying, her mascara and makeup already running down her face. She knew Kellie just as well as I did. She was a second mom to her.

The police officer turned to my mom. "We currently have no leads on how she was murdered, but I promise you we will get to the bottom of this, there will be a funeral and memorial service for her on..." I stopped paying attention, and at that moment, everything stopped. I knew I was still sitting there, but my mind has felt like it has halted. I felt so broken, and an unrepairable sadness took over me. I couldn't even cry, I just sat there as the police officer's mouth continued moving, but I could hear no sound come out of her mouth. They must find the person who murdered my sweet, pure Kellie. She would never have done anything to hurt a soul. How could someone do this to her? I wanted to scream and shout at the woman, as there must be more that she can do. However, I sat there staring at her moving lips, not knowing how to fix the pain in my heart, knowing I will never see, hear, or talk to my dear best friend anymore.

A month later, I was lying in my bed, staring up at the ceiling, the dull pain in my chest aching more than it ever has. Just two months ago, I was lying on this same bed with Kellie, staring up at the ceiling. Kellie was going on about how my popcorn ceiling reminded her of pimples. I laughed and told her that if every "pimple" on my ceiling were somehow on her face, she would still look like a beautiful goddess. She shook her head and smiled, unsure how to take the compliment. I smiled at the memory and knew that if she were here right now, she would be telling me of my pimple ceiling and how I should get rid of it.

"I know now that I will never get rid of my pimple ceiling," I whispered to myself as a single tear slowly rolled down my cheek. "Even if-"

An abrupt knock sounded at our front door, losing my train of thought. I wiped my tears and slowly got out of my bed, and walked into the living room. My mom got up and answered the door, and to our surprise, the same police officer that informed us of Kellie's murder was standing in the doorway. I stood up straighter, intrigued by what she had to say. Did they find her murderer? It has been almost a month, and they have not seemed to be getting any closer to finding the monster who destroyed the pure soul of Kellie Peters.

"Hi there Ms. Ross, unfortunately we have not found the

culprit, but my team is working extra hard to get to the bottom of the case. I have a few questions to ask your daughter that will help our team if that's okay," she glanced at me, and a shudder ran down my spine. Her eyes were cold and intense. When she turned back to my mom, she gave a small smile.

My mom nodded and turned to let her in the door. She motioned to her to have a seat on the couch, and I followed.

"Hi Caroline, these questions shouldn't take long, and I want you to know you have nothing to worry about. Our team will use these questions to understand more vividly what happened that night." I nodded, and she continued. "So, I will start by asking, where were you the night of August 27th, 2019?

My mind wandered to a month ago. I explained that I was picking up Kellie to go to a party, but she wanted to go with some other friends, and so I ended up not going at all.

The police officer nodded while scribbling words into a handheld notebook. "Where did you go instead of the party?"

I hesitated. I went to Kellie's house to ask her if she should really go to the party with those friends, but I mustn't tell her that. "I-I went back home," my heart is now racing, and my fingers are going numb.

She glanced at me from her notebook and started writing more. "And would you say you were jealous of her newfound friends?"

"Well, no, of course not. She can have friends of her own, I just didn't think they were good for her and I wanted to make sure she was okay," I winced. I didn't mean to tell her that.

"What do you mean you wanted to make sure she was okay?"

"Well I went to her house for a little bit before she left," my words barely coming out of my quickened breaths. "I wanted to make sure she really wanted to leave with them." Was what I did so wrong? Jessica would've done anything to get the attention of any senior jock, and she should know that she would leave her the second after he does.

"Why didn't you tell me that earlier?" She questioned with a hint of suspicion.

"I-I d-don't know," I stuttered.

The police officer thought for a moment. "As the only witness before Jessica Haney showed up on the scene, you are now the prime suspect and I have to put you under arrest."

My eyes widened, and I couldn't breathe. My mother started yelling as handcuffs were locked around my wrists. All I could think about Kellie's silent cries for help as her breaths stopped under the pressure of my palms around her throat. "I-I didn't mean to hurt her. I-I'm sorry."

The Tale of The Starving Girl

By Lizzie Adams (Finalist)

Once, there was a young girl named Peony. She was a shy girl who spent most of her life at an old hospital. She was born weak, vulnerable to any sort of illness, leaving her to be bedridden for the first few years of her life.

Every day was the same. The nurses would take some of the children outside at least once a day to get as much sun as possible. Peony wished to go outside like the other children, but couldn't due to her condition. Until one day, one nurse rolled her bed out onto the lawn. Peony had never felt so happy in her life.

She loved that nurse, for she cared for her and got her whatever she needed- food, water, even medicine to help with her condition. Peony especially loved the hospital's cook and her food. The cook's dishes were made with absolute perfection, and they were believed to give the patients the strength they needed to recover. But the cook's most famous dish was a hearty stew, filled with meat and vegetables. Peony loved it because the meat was unlike anything she ever tried before. She didn't know what kind of meat it was, but she loved the taste of it.

The day came when Peony could finally wander out of her bed. She had recovered enough to finally play outside with the other children, but she was still being monitored in case her condition weakened again. A few of the children had gotten well enough to finally leave the hospital, but she and a few others remained. The nurse allowed Peony to explore any area of the hospital she wished, but there was one rule: never go into the pantry.

A month went on, and Peony obeyed without question. She wandered around the different rooms in the hospital, never getting bored. She played outside with the other children like normal. Peony lived a mostly happy life.

One day, one of the children, a girl whom Peony often played with, was called to be taken home. They said their goodbyes, and then she left. Dinner was even lonelier than usual, and for some reason the rich stew Peony loved didn't feel as comforting like it normally did.

At midnight, Peony woke feeling hungry. She crawled out of bed and crept into the hall, straight towards the kitchen. She hid among the shadows as to not be seen by the cook, who appeared to be cleaning her knife. She came close to approaching the door to the pantry. She knew it was forbidden, but her hunger and curiosity had gotten the better of her; she was at least hoping to find something to snack on, then return to bed.

So she slowly lifted the latch of the door, and went into the pantry. It was dark, and the floor felt cold and wet under her feet. The stench of meat filled the air. Peony couldn't see a thing in the small, cramped room, so she took out a candle she had in her pocket and lit it. In the dim light, she could see that the floor was stained with red. There were cuts of meat on the shelves and the floor, but they looked unfamiliar, less like any livestock that was ever butchered. Then she saw a familiar lock of hair. One closer look, and she could see the face of her friend: pale, with grey lifeless eyes.

Peony was horrified. Was this what really happened to the children who supposedly went home? Was this what the cook had been putting into the hospital's meals this whole time? Would she be next?

Suddenly, she heard footsteps. There was nowhere to hide. She had disobeyed the nurse she once admired, and now she had to either find a way to escape or face the consequences.

The door slowly opened, and a sharp gleam of metal shone...

Quiet Familiarity

By Hannah Hoover (Finalist)

I woke up on a stone-cold floor. How long have I been asleep? That doesn't matter now I just need to get out. But first I have to find out how and also when. After several days in my cell, I've figured out the general guard schedule by listening to the sounds of feet echoing on the stone surface of the walls and floors outside. Luckily, they seem to only come up and down the hall during mealtimes and lights out. So I'll have plenty of unguarded time to dig, scrape, or whatever I decide to do.

My cell has an iron door on it with a barred window at the top and a food slot at the bottom. On the opposite wall is a window to the outside with more bars. I also have a bed that is bolted to the floor and a bedpan-looking thing that I've been assuming is used for a bathroom. Digging wasn't much of an option since the floor was made of stone as well and trying to get through that would cause more noise than I could make without raising suspicion.

Between lunch and dinner one day, I did a thorough inspection of the bars on the window to the outside. I discovered that one of the bars was already loose. I decided to start working on getting the remaining bars out as well. It took several days but I did get enough bars out to get out of the cell.

Once outside, I took a look around and realized that I stood in a large maze and that the building that I had been housed in was nowhere to be found. I wandered for a long while and made it to what I would venture was the middle of the maze. I sat on a bench that was there and thought about how I had made it to this point. Where had my cell gone and where was I now? I almost wished for the quiet familiarity of the cell. However, I did not know where it was so my only option was to keep moving through the maze. Though I had a few dead ends after an hour or so I found myself out of the maze.

Instead of any sort of indication that other human life existed outside of the maze, I was greeted with the ocean. It was calm and sprayed a salty mist onto my face that wasn't entirely unpleasant. I walked along the shore to see if I could find anyone but I could not. I looked for food, for I was becoming hungry, but I found none.

Eventually, I found myself back at the maze. I went back in and found my way to the middle. I sat once again on the bench. Glancing about I knew that I had seen this before but it was not welcoming to be here. I rose again to look for the building.

Several hours passed but I found it. I climbed back through the window and replaced the bars. Then sat quietly and waited for the next meal. When it came I heard the guard say, ""Glad to have you back,"" in a condescending voice. I simply sat and smiled softly at the familiar walls that had never seen quite so welcoming.

Eden of Igo

By Rosabella Debty (Finalist)

It had only been fifteen minutes. Fifteen minutes from the time she had entered the market to the time she had been thrown into a cell. Hell had come to earth fifteen minutes ago, and she let it happen.

She felt the time tick in her head, second by second, as she was left quiet in her thoughts. The only sound that kept her grounded to reality was the soft trickle of water through some ungodly pipe in the ceiling. With every swish and gulp the metal took, she pictured all of the chemicals and waste that went down its open throat.

A laugh come to her at the imagery, of a great, big monster that had a stomach pathed to the ocean, forever processing the shit that her government fed it. Jay was probably four cells down with the same thought.

Jay.

The two were supposed to stay together when they tore into the crowd, though she should've known that plan would fail. After the riots had begun, she no longer saw him beside her, no longer heard his shouting. Maybe he had been able to escape before they came in with their automatic guns and camouflaged boots, shooting down anyone in their way. Maybe he didn't have to sit in the damp, musty smelling cell wondering the beast's name in the faucet.

She would do it all over again, if given the option, even if she received the same outcome. Their message was out there now, broadcasted all over Paven, maybe even the nation.

She heard a creak in her door and opened her eyes, no longer allowed in her own thoughts as two security guards walked over to cuff her hands where she sat. Usually she would've said a witty remark, but wasting them on henchmen wasn't her goal. They didn't speak as they moved into the new room, one that was bright and sterile and had two chairs on opposite sides of a table. She felt the beady eyes that stared behind the two-way mirror she faced.

She was left alone again, sitting in her spot at the table that was too white to be realistic. Looking up at the mirror, she winked towards whoever stood behind it with a wide grin.

A clock on the wall marked that it had now been two hours and seventeen minutes since the market, and that she no longer had to follow an internal clock.

"Indigo Torez." She heard the voice before she saw the man, dressed in black and gripping a now crinkled folder. The door slammed shut behind him as he strode to the seat paralleling hers. "Known as Indie by friends and Igo by followers." He wasn't unattractive, though his years showed through his receding hairline and the creases that ran parallel above his brows.

"And which one are you, mister?" Her voice was foreign to her now, a little raspy from yelling the few hours before and having been silent through the rest.

A small chuckle came from the man, opening the file in front of him. "Detective Peters, and while I'm sure you would love to be buddy buddy with me, that's not how our relationship has been mapped out."

"Oh, bummer. I was already making charm bracelets." She pouted for dramatic affect, trying to ignore the feeling of her cuffs digging into her skin. There would definitely be bruising if not marks for a little while.

"'What were you doing in Wicker Cove, Ms. Torez?" He seemed to know her game, the angle she was playing.

"Does it not say in that mountain of a file you have?"

"I want to hear it from you."

Indigo clenched her jaw, looking over to the mirror again. She felt her lip curl over her teeth, unable to stop the laugh that bubbled in her throat and reverberated around the blank room.

"Well, since you asked so nicely," She murmured, letting her eyes train back onto the detective, "The public deserved to know."

"Deserved to know what?"

"Everything. The planet's failing. Our president sits in his billion dollar home, watching the rest of us die off like ants. We have no money, no food, and no plan to receive either anytime soon. We have floating transportation and vaccines that cure cancer, but we have no birds, no trees." She leaned in as far as her cuffs would allow, seething. "And most importantly, we have no choice."

They had no choice on any matter. Their silver speech was stained gold, their actions created by puppeteers. They lived in the garden of eden, and their president was playing God. Every possibility was open, as long as one didn't eat from the fruit of knowledge.

Though, if the president was God, Indigo was the snake.

Eternal Memory

By Ariyanna Donley (Finalist)

An alarm sounds. Ophelia wakes up, and with a blaring headache, turns off the alarm and tiredly sits up. Ophelia's morning routine does not consist of much, as she hasn't been outside in over a year after developing agoraphobia. Thanks to her roommate Anwir, Ophelia has been able to enjoy the comfort of her home.

As Ophelia goes to turn on her bathroom sink, she notices a light bruise on her wrist,

"When did this happen?" She thinks to herself. Opening her cabinet she grabs an Advil for her headache and finishes up. Exiting her room, Ophelia greets her roommate Anwir, who is in the kitchen cooking breakfast. She takes in the sweet smell of pancakes and bacon, until she notices the beer bottles on the small dining room table in the corner.

"Dude, how much did you drink last night? There's like 8

bottles here," Ophelia scoffs while grabbing one of the bottles and sitting down.

Laughing, Anwir says, "You think I could do that alone, you drank some too." Putting his spatula down he turns toward her and smirks "you've got a headache, don't you?"

"What? Anwir... You know I don't drink"

Anwir stares back at Ophelia, he smiles again, "How so? I convinced you to last night."

Shrugging and turning back to the food, Anwir says, "I see why you stopped in the first place, you went all crazy about feeling trapped and started breaking everything, I basically had to tie you down until you fell asleep."

Ophelia goes silent, in disbelief over the embarrassing moment she must've caused the night before. Finished with cooking the food, Anwir softly sets a plate in front of Ophelia, watching her in a trance. Hearing the plate set on the table, Ophelia snaps out of it, and turns towards the table. The two hungrily eat their food, making small talk in between bites.

After eating, Ophelia makes her way into the living room, and plops herself down on the couch. Looking around the room, Ophelia sits up and yells into the kitchen "Have you seen my laptop?"

Anwir yells back, "Yeah it's in here, I'll bring it."

Relaxing herself into the couch, Ophelia waits for Anwir to bring her laptop. She checks her phone, 10 minutes passed. Impatiently, Ophelia gets up, and when she does, Anwir walks into the room carrying her laptop in his hands.

"Jeez, what took you so long?" Ophelia asks, taking the laptop out of Anwir's hands.

"Sorry, I must've misplaced it"

"Well stop touching my stuff, and maybe you won't"

"Wow, rude much, I didn't even use it, I just moved it last night, so you wouldn't break it during your little tantrum."

"Whatever," Ophelia says, rolling her eyes, and sitting back down on the couch.

"You should believe me more often, it would be better for you." Anwir snaps back, walking out of the room.

Ignoring him, Ophelia opens her laptop. Excited to do some digital design work, she opens her design folder.

"Huh, the files missing," Ophelia thinks to herself, scurrying through all of her folders to find it. "Maybe I deleted it."

Ophelia goes to her recently deleted folder, and, as she suspected, finds the file.

However, she also finds a video with the exact same name in the folder as well. Wondering what it could be, Ophelia opens the video and begins to watch it. About 15 minutes later,

Anwir enters the room, after calming down from their argument earlier, he remembers he's gotta keep his eye on her.

"Hey, what are you watching?" Anwir asks, peeking over Ophelia's shoulder.

Ophelia jumps and slams the computer shut. "Nothing! I

was just watching myself review some of my old designs." Ophelia says, wiping away a tear from her cheek.

Anwir goes silent for a moment, watching Ophelia wipe her tears, he remarks "Why are you crying then? You're always so emotional."

Forcing a laugh, Ophelia says "You know how I am, I was just reminiscing on how far I've come."

"Yeah I do know," Anwir replies, "how about a movie? It'll take your mind off of things."

"Sounds good. You stay here, I'll go to the kitchen and make some popcorn," Ophelia answers, getting up and rushing towards the kitchen.

Ophelia bursts into the kitchen, and throws a bag of popcorn into the microwave. She checks into the living room and sees that Anwir is sitting on the couch. Hurriedly, she turns back around, and grabs a knife out of the kitchen drawer. With the knife behind her back, she runs back towards the living room, but is surprised to see that Anwir has disappeared. Slowly, Ophelia walks towards the couch, "Anwir, this isn't funny, stop joking around." She reaches the couch, and sees that Anwir is not laying there.

Feeling a presence behind her, Ophelia quickly turns around, but is too late. Anwir stabs Ophelia in the neck with a medical needle, injecting her with a mysterious fluid.

"Anwir, how could you do this? Ophelia says as she grabs Anwir's arm.

Catching Ophelia before she hits the floor, Anwir replies,

"I'm sorry Ophelia, looks like today was another failure."

Ophelia scoffs, "No wonder I can't remember anything, how long have I been stuck here?"

"About a year, but Ophelia, I have no choice, this experiment could change the world"

Anwir urges. "All I have to do is completely stop you from regaining your memory, and it'll be complete. I've been a bit lazy lately haven't I Ophelia? I'll do better next tomorrow, you won't remember a single thing," Anwir smiles, brushing Ophelia's hair out of her face.

Losing the energy to argue, Ophelia's vision begins to fade, "You won't get away with this."

"Oh? Why not? I've got the government on my side."

Ophelia passes out. An alarm sounds. Ophelia wakes up, and with a blaring headache, turns off the alarm and tiredly sits up.

A Dark Halloween

By Alexia Davis (Finalist)

It was a mysterious October night, the time of night that trick-or-treaters would be getting ready for their huge night of staying up late, eating candy, and getting drunk off of way too much apple cider. This is the night where people watch enough scary movies to the point that they are scared for the rest of the month. The night where no one wants to stay in their house, afraid that they will miss a split second of the fun. The cold, crisp air was the perfect weather for the holiday season. The children on the street of Burbonville would be going around in their costumes of ghosts, goblins, and vampires scaring others into giving them all of their candy.

Going to the kitchen, I lay out the chocolate bars for all of the children that will pass by my doorstep. Hopefully, they will enjoy it this year instead of the apples that I passed out last year. It took me until Christmas to find all of the toilet paper that they threw onto my house. The only good thing about it is that I had free toilet paper, not that I used it for that reason because that would be disgusting. Putting last year behind me I was determined that this year was going to be different. I was going to be the popular house among the children. The house that they all wanted to go to. The house that reminds you of why you wanted to go trick-or-treating in the first place.

I went to my bedroom to put on my Halloween costume, so excited to show the kids. Looking in my closet, trying to figure out where I put it, I caught a glimpse of green glitter in the back of the closet. Pulling out the green glittery costume, I put it on and instantly embraced the beautiful fairy I desired to be. Looking in the mirror, I felt as if I could fly around the room using the fake wings that I had put on, but alas if I were to do that some bone would be broken. Bustling with anticipation, I ran out of my bedroom and back into the kitchen.

Ding Dong. I heard from the front door. I knew that this must be my first trick-or-treater of the night. I grabbed my bowl of chocolate and ran up to the door instantly swinging it open only to find that it was the postman. He looked at me with open confusion and disgust holding a package I must have ordered when I was half asleep, I truly had no idea what in the world was going on.

"Nice pixie outfit," he said looking me up and down one more time. After signing the package that I acquired, I went to the kitchen and sat at the table, hoping desperately the next person that came through the door would be dressed as their favorite princess or villain with a huge pearly white smile on their face.

Minutes of waiting turned into hours. I began to become worried. Were these children not getting the candy that they deserved? Did they not like me? How can I make up for last year if no one comes to visit me? I wondered. I walked outside expecting to see children laughing and chasing each other around, but instead, I found the street of Burbonville completely dead and dull.

Empty? I thought. How could such a busy street be empty? I've been waiting with my chocolate bars forever for these kids to show up. The street can't be empty, on this wonderful night filled with creatures hidden in the shadows. It was so empty that you could hear the crows cooing in the distance, the wind howling up a storm. You could feel the trees shaking slightly as the wind combed through their reddish-orange leaves. All the lights in the jack-o'-lanterns were blown out by a huge gust of wind. My neighbor's doors were tightly locked, but I didn't know why.

I walked up and down the street wondering if I was missing out. I had to be. No one could be seen for miles. Why is it so quiet on one of the most festive nights of the year? Where are the smiles and laughter? Could it be because of ghosts or goblins like stories speak of? Or maybe the witches are traveling through the night once more. I reach for the phone out of fear for myself and catch a glimpse of something so shocking, so scary, it almost gave me a heart attack, the calendar. I drop the phone in relief, only to find out that it is October 30th.

A Cold War and a Crimson Ledger

By Shirley Lachance (Finalist)

Amelia Lenkov was lying on her green threadbare couch staring at the dingy blue wallpaper of her fourth story studio apartment. It was 1958, she had just spent a long day at the office. As secretary for the head of the Department of Defense, Amelia knew it was her job to conceal the top secret information that was disclosed to her. When she came home each day, Amelia would clear her mind with a glass, or two, of wine. Eleven chimes from the Old Post Office clock tower echoed outside her D.C. apartment. Her glass of wine sat on the oak end table, the slightest dregs of her pinot noir lingering at the bottom of the glass. Moonlight shone through her window, reflecting off the crystal wine glass. The light danced around the room, decorating the otherwise bare walls. Just as Amelia began to drift off to sleep, CRASH! The window and the wine glass shattered, spraying all over the room. The bullet missed her by millimeters — grabbing her pistol and jacket she scrambled out of the door.

The twilight chill nipped at the nape of her neck, the shooter was nowhere to be seen. This was to be expected, she thought to herself, and began to go inside. However, just before she stepped in the front door Amelia looked up at her window. The window was intact. There was no bullet hole in her wall and no broken window where there had been moments before. As she walked out into the street, the wind blew her curly chestnut hair across her face. She pushed it away looking up at her window "four up and three to the right, four up and three to the right" she murmured to herself. Now standing in the middle of 11th Street she could see her wine glass sitting on her end table. It was then that she heard a faint, soft, almost cooing, voice singing a Russian lullaby. She recognized the song as one that her mother used to sing to her as a child. The voice grew louder, deafening. Suddenly, a bright light flashed and Amelia was gone.

She awoke hours later — getting her bearings she could hear waves crashing and felt sand between her fingers and toes. Amelia shivered in the absence of her warm burgundy coat. She watched the condensation from her breath floating through the air. Suddenly, a shrieking maniacal laugh echoed on the shore. Paralyzed, Amelia realized she wasn't alone. It was a laugh she knew all too well, and one she hoped to never hear again.

"Dimitri, my darling. How long has it been?..." Amelia looked up at the slender shadow of the man she knew to be her former employer and lover. Dimitri drew nearer. He was a tall, pale man with jet black hair, and golden brown eyes. His presence was almost ghostlike.

"Too long my dear. Did you think you could run from your past forever? I'm the only one who knows what you really are."

"I didn't run or hide. I just wanted nothing to do with you." Amelia snarled. She'd left Russia at the beginning of the Cold War. Once the war started, the "business" became too much, even for her. Yet, once again she found herself trapped by the life she thought she had left behind in St. Petersburg.

Amelia couldn't afford for the U.S. government to find out about her powers, or to know her true identity. But standing before her was the man who knew all her secrets. It was clear, she could no longer stay out of this war. She'd have to fight. Amelia didn't know for what side or for how long. She did know destruction would follow her, and that her pale hands were about to be dripping in red, darkening her already crimson ledger.

False Dreams

By Abbie McCollum (Finalist)

My alarm goes off, it's 9:00am.

It's March 4, 1934. Everything is right in the world. Everything peaceful and quiet. Not a soul being harmed, and everyone is okay.

I get out of bed, make it up, and get ready for the day. I have plans to go outside and fix the garden as well as to go to the store.

I wear the pink dress that is all the way in the back of my closet. It looks good with my brown hair and eyes. I wear it with some nice sandals and my favorite ring. I do my make up really nice and curl my hair.

Later, I go downstairs to eat breakfast quickly so I can get to work. I finish my cereal and wash my dishes and go out the door. I get started in the garden, planting some new flowers and vegetables. Chamomiles are my favorite, but I don't let anyone know because I don't want to seem weird.

"Hey Rosie!" I hear my friend call from the other side of the gate. His name is Luke Haney. He's been my friend since fourth grade but he wasn't supposed to be back from his trip until late April. We will graduate together in about three months.

"Hi, Luke!" I smile and wave. He looks a little different from the last time I saw him. He came to celebrate Christmas with our family and left afterwards. He has blondish hair, skin is a little dark, eyes a nice blue and he's wearing his usual yellow hoodie.

He walks over to me and gives me a hand with watering the newly planted flowers. "I've come back a little earlier than expected." He says.

"Yeah, I see." I respond, smiling. "I wasn't expecting anyone to come here. Thanks for the help." I take the watering can from his hands.

"Don't mention it." He smiles. "You still look lovely I see." We both stand up, but he helps me. "Is there anything else you need to do today?" He asks.

"Thanks for the complement and yes, but all of which I can handle on my own." I remove my hand from his and clean up my area. "Would you like something to drink? I cannot stay for long, but you can make yourself at home."

He nods and I lead him inside. We sit down at the table and I pour him some lemonade. I accidentally spill some onto the table.

"I'll get some paper towels." Luke says as he gets up.

I'm usually not this clumsy. I guess it's just because Luke is here when I was least expecting him to come.

He comes back and cleans up the mess. "You know, I don't think I've ever seen you spill this much before. I mean, I remember the time you had a crush on some guy at school and you were pouring yourself a drink and he came over to talk to you but- "

"I know what happened." I cut him off and sit down on the couch.

He drinks his lemonade and comes to sit by me. "You know, if you hurry up and get motivated, I can drive you into town and you can go do what you need to do." He smiles and looks at me.

"I can handle myself, Luke. You know this." I look back at him.

"Yes, this I do know already, but what's so wrong about me helping you? Let's go." He says and grabs my hand, taking me out to his car.

I get in not willing to fight with him any longer. He chuckles and starts the car. "Where to?" He asks.

"I need to go to the store and pick up a few things." I respond as he starts driving.

He looks at me and back to the road. He continues driving, occasionally looking back at me. "You're being awfully quiet, Rosie."

"You're the only one who calls me that."

"I can fix that."

"I rather you didn't"

"Fix it or call you Rosie."

I don't respond, instead I look out of the window. He keeps driving and eventually gets tired of the silence.

"Rosie." He says.

"Yes, Luke?"

"What's wrong?"

"There is nothing wrong. I'm fine, I just have a lot of things I need to do." I look over at him and smile.

"Okay." He smiles back.

"I'm sorry, Luke, for being so mean earlier."

"It's fine, Rosie," he grabs my hand and plays with the ring he gave me last summer, "I still love you." I smile and look out the window again.

I fall asleep along the ride, not worrying because I know Luke knows how to drive and he won't let anything happen to me. I'm fine so long as I have Luke by my side. My only best friend. The one I love.

My alarm goes off, it's 9:00am.

It's March 4, 1934. It will be a busy day; I have plans to go outside and fix the garden as well as to go to the store.

Run

By Evelyn Rodriguez (Finalist)

Two hours, forty minutes, thirty nine point eighteen seconds.
That's how long it took Angelina to realize she was being
followed. How would I know? Well that's simple, I'm the one
following her. She hides what I seek, that's how it goes. A
precious item, a jewel or a necklace you might think. But no, I'm
after something much more valuable. I'm after that queen bee,
that tattered cloth girl, that human.

I walk and I walk and I walk and

I walk and I walk and I walk and

I walk and I walk and I walk and

I walk and I walk and I walk and

I walk and I walk and I walk and

I walk and I walk and I walk and

I walk and I walk and I walk and

I walk and I walk and I walk and

I walk and I walk and I walk

Can she see me? I'm not sure, but I hope she can. She makes my heart tingle, it's funny what love makes you do. I even put together the life she so longed for. One of children and happiness and joy and, and me.

I run and I run and I run and

I run and I run and I run and

I run and I run and I run and

I run and I run and I run and

I run and I run and I run and

I run and I run and I run and

I run and I run and I run and

I run and I run and I run and

I run and I run and I run

You can hear the voices too can't you. The ones that don't care or smile back. So what if those voices are gone. They can't get you anymore. I should know, I got rid of them.

I sprint and I sprint and I sprint and

I sprint and I sprint and I sprint and

I sprint and I sprint and I sprint and

I sprint and I sprint and I sprint and

I sprint and I sprint and I sprint and

I sprint and I sprint and I sprint and

I sprint and I sprint and I sprint and

I sprint and I sprint and I sprint

No more running.

Cool Imagination Titles

Convergence by Brian Claspell
Jim Conrad may not be as fictional as the CIA thinks. Pick up *Convergence*, a mystery-thriller, on Amazon and at other fine retailers.

One Spark - Short Story Anthology 2011-2018
Enjoy reading the short stories of all the winners (2011-2018) and 2018 finalist of the "Imagination Begins with You..." high school writing contest. All proceeds support scholarships.

One Spark – "Imagination Begins with You..." 2019
Jump into reading finalist stories from the "Imagination Begins with You..." high school writing contest. All proceeds support scholarships.

One Spark – "Imagination Begins with You..." 2020
"Imagination Begins with You..." high school writing contest is an annual writing contest open. The finalist and winners are published in an annual short story collection where all proceeds support scholarships. Enjoy!

One Spark – "Imagination Begins with You..." 2021
Full of amazing stories from young writers in the "Imagination Begins with You..." high school writing contest. 100% of proceeds support writing scholarships.

www.ingramcontent.com/pod-product-compliance
Lightning Source LLC
Chambersburg PA
CBHW031134210626
46816CB00014B/707